GOODBYE SOBER DAY

ROBERT MONDAY

NEWMAN SPRINGS PUBLISHING
320 Broad Street
Red Bank, NJ 07701

First originally published by Newman Springs Publishing 2023

ISBN 979-8-88763-427-2 (Paperback)
ISBN 979-8-88763-428-9 (Digital)

Printed in the United States of America

To My Mother and Father

Come, let us make a hell of our own, and
try how long we can bear it.
A good dream is better than a bad reality.

—Blackbeard

A Bit of an Introduction

And there they were, dressed as red skeletons to honor the flag of the rapscallion Edward Low, the sadist of the seas and existential anarchist—Boston's own bastard pyrate.

The Bible says, your eyes will see strange things, and your heart utter perverse things.

At their shows, they bear-paw their instruments, frolicking on stage like demon spawn, all the while hailing the advantages of jungle law that they set to a lyrical flow within the genre of the punk rock rhythm.

At their shows, they decree themselves as chaos-embodying terrorists of the maritime variety. Real salty dogs, with enough cock in their rock to scare the tits off your father and invert your whole Christian reality. They admit as much, prefacing the onset of each of their shows with punk pyrate proclamations.

"You cunts can all stop your cheering right now 'cause before the night is over, we are going to put our grubby hands all over your booty and commence to burning your unmarred Jolly Roger!"

The front man says this as he brandishes a lit Zippo, and then in a wobbly English accent, he announces the name of their skeleton crew, "Y'all ready to be Fuck'd for Life?"

Get it? Skeleton crew?

For those of you unfamiliar with the expressions used from those of the scallywag vocation, to rip or to burn another crew's Jolly Roger is the gravest of insults and signifies an act of all-out war. And of course, you can rest assured that "booty," in this case, refers to valuables like cash and jewelry—treasures that a bastard pyrate might try relieving a victim of.

The band, however, is not implying any intention of forcibly manhandling anyone's posterior.

Or are they? Sometimes it's hard to tell with these goofballs. Either way, you should possibly consider sleeping on your backside tonight.

At their shows, they typically kick things off by playing either "Consume" or "Pyrate Statesman." Both songs are off their album, Low and Lawless.

"Kill your boss! Kill your boss!"

Did you know that Edward Low was described by Sir Arthur Conan Doyle, the creator of Sherlock Holmes, as "a man of amazing and grotesque brutality"? He said Low was both "savage and desperate."

"Not a loss! Not a loss to kill your boss!"

Of course, you didn't know that.

"Rape his wife! End his life!"

Did you know that Edward Low, the bastard pyrate, was scarred at the mouth, like a sort of half-complete Glasgow smile?

"Chop off his fucking legs! Even if he begs!"

Did you know that he sailed a ship called the Merry Christmas?

"Bind his kids with electrical wire…"

Did you know the bastard was particularly fond of torture and forced cannibalism?

"Then set his fucking house on fire!"

Did you know he forced victims to eat their own broiled lips?

"Low and lawless! This plan was flawless! Killing for solace."

Then the bassist and drummer, with accompanying vocals, join in. **"Then as he's crying and wailing and bleeding, trying to save his kids or wife, or maybe he said 'fuck it' and now he's trying to slither to the door, you grab him by his bloody fucking nubs, you fucking jerk off on his fucking stupid fucking forehead.**

"Low and lawless! Killing for solace! Low and lawless! Killing for solace! Killing for solace! Killing for solace! Killing for solace! Killing for solace!"

Did you know that the bastard pyrate Low started his career by declaring a war on humanity?

Then the front man will end the song with a deadpan, **"We are Fuck'd for Life, and we support this message!"**

And he really puts his body and being into this delivery. It happens, of course, in tandem with the bassist and drummer putting real fucking heat into giving the end of the song the proper punctuation. Boom!

At the end of his career, Ed Low was running out of men that would sail the seas with him as his cruelties aboard the vessels were getting worse, so he was reduced to running a skeleton crew.

Did you know that?

At their shows, on stage and in between their songs, this aggressive little punk band dressed as red skeletons. They would chug acrid booze and espouse misanthropic slogans: "This is the best night of your pathetic lives, you big boring beige turds!" and "Don't forget to buy our CDs because the subliminal messages telling youse to kill yourselves need to be heard by all of youse!"

Liner notes: Savage (drums), Erik J. Worthley (bass), and Classic Nick (guitar and lead vocals). Referred to affectionally amongst themselves as "the boys."

*****

July 13, 1999. The album *California* by Mr. Bungle is released, instantly becoming a new obsession with the boys playing it all the damn time. On the night of the twenty-second of the same month, the Blunderbus cruising on the I-90 W in New York, the boys take turns firing upon other vehicles with their paintball guns. The bassist, utilizing the fire escape in the roof, climbed on top of their spray-painted special-needs bus to fire two hundred red paintballs at whatever corporate rock star's million-dollar tour bus they just passed on the right. The three boys, thoroughly cocaine-fed, scream, singing "Goodbye Sober Day" just as Mike Patton screams "Goodbye sober day" while the song blares from within the Blunderbus. The song would become their official song of the summer, and perhaps their unofficial song of the year.

*****

It was definitely around springtime when the after-parties at the house got more COLOURFUL. It's hard to keep track as we are always fucked up, so they all sort of blend together.

(Grant me the vision, Dr. Zeus. Grant me the vision with my sacred juice!)

We would have a machete into a Magnavox television. This, if it's still plugged in, will spark and pop and smoke. In our backyard firepit, we burn the destroyed bits of unloved furniture. We take turns stomping the TV because TV ruins more lives than heroin. We sing our songs off-key and full volume as we launch fireworks. And one time, one of us even had a flare gun that we shot at each other that we deflected with the metal lids from our trash cans. Star Child is the name of the machete, and now they're using it to hew more of our expendable possessions—mostly the glass, ceramic, and wooden shit. They do this while I play hype man with a megaphone and declare the destruction a sacrifice to our weird gods.

(I wanna be a rock god here!) You tell yourself the behavior isn't indicative of something larger. It's nothing diagnosable, the way you live. It's a philosophy—after all, I am in my twenties. *(I wanna be a rock god there!)* Isn't the rock and roll lifestyle compulsory, especially when one is in a band? *(Rock god, I am pyrate as I jam!)* That must be a bylaw or some kind of archaic statute. Read the fine print of life, people!

We dance around the wine and drink red fire. We do this under the moon that thick clouds make to look like it's frothy, like the head of a dark beer. "Page 6" by Fantômas plays as we piss behind the garage. We do bumps of coke off a plastic plectrum that says D.A.R.E. on it that someone brought but no one is quite sure who. "We gotta dare the darers to do some damn drugs!" The combination of cocaine and alcohol makes our eyes demon-glare. Our eyes are big and black, like an owl's (this happens in seconds), and then we stare at each other as we quote sinister lyrics from our favorite evil songs while, at the same time, picking the same Sonic Youth song.

I dump my goblet of wine over Savage's head. "Main Title" (White and Lazy) by John Zorn's Filmworks 1986–1990 plays, and we jump over the fire and dance the dance of the psychotic. Rite of

Spring with a twist. Danse Macabre with the Macarena. We dance like we don't know the rules and we just want to do our own goddamn thing. We play industrial rock on our acoustic instruments and listen to tribal music on our industrial speakers.

Erik shows me weird gold coins he says he stole today from someone's house; they catch the fire as he finger-flips the biggest one. He says, from now on, no more paper currency. He's only about hard metal. We laugh. We listen to Antonio Vivaldi's *The Four Seasons.*

Those Asian girls from Smith College that bought our shirts come over again, and they are wearing our shirts. These girls travel in thick clouds of elite pussy pheromones, and they take turns fucking us on the backyard grass. It is mid-spring, but the ground is still cold, so they ask for wool blankets.

Concerto no. 1 in E major, op. 8, RV 269, "Spring" (*La primavera*) is the first in Vivaldi's arrangement. We fuck beside low-tempo strobe lights, and throughout the night, we keep shouting funny slogans on how we are doing all this to honor our twenty-first-century versions of the ancient gods and how this is achieved with lunacy, alcoholism, and rock and roll. But in reality, we are doing this for our twentieth-century rock and roll gods, and this is achieved with lunacy, alcoholism, and rock and roll.

"Heaven/Hell" by Chumbawamba plays.

The three of us look up at the moon. Bare tree branches lend perspective.

The goal is to always take it up a notch.

Erik shouts, "There is evidence in the Bible that Satan has time-traveling abilities!" He is shouting this as he lies on the grass while a Russian stripper squats over him and pisses in his face.

Savage has the megaphone and is asking if there are any dames here tonight that want to shove the stem of a lollipop into his cock and then blow him. "There's gum in the center."

Maybe over the years, I lost my soul—lost it in the bottle. And perhaps this is why we call the contents "spirits."

I ask the busty dame with giant eyes, "What kind of accent is that?"

She says, "My parents are from Mexico and Vatican City."

She is wearing a Hampshire College sweater that I point to. "What's your major?"

She smiles. "My goal is to be the biggest name in American adult entertainment."

"What's your porn name?"

"Naughty Habit. I specialize in nun porno."

Smash cut! to however many minutes later, and she's got her fake tits out, and me and some fag in an Amherst College sweater are jerking off on her. She tells us to bukkake on her crucifix necklace. "Cum on Jesús." And she pronounces it like "Hay-Seuss."

Afterward, Savage tells me, "Yeah, she's got a dick. His name was Jesús." He belches. "I think it is Bethany now or some shit." He laughs. "Yeah, she's a trickster, that one. Erik and I JO'd on her last week. I think Erik knew the whole time, ya know. He likes that religious porno." He belches again, then pops a handful of pills. "Hey, what kind of fish do priests eat on Fridays? *Nun!* Get it?"

We do the *Uncle Buck dance* to "Common People" by Pulp while a midget dressed as a gargoyle jumps off the roof onto some douche with a Barenaked Ladies T-shirt and fucking knocks him out cold. We then bribe the *little devil* with a bag of coke to shit on his head. Kodak moment!

Drugs are always around. I remember, in school, they said drug dealers' goals were to hook you so they can have a customer for life, but I don't think we've *paid* for any drugs all year. So fuck teachers. They're retarded.

We hold flashlights under our chins and chase some skittish Connecticut broads around the backyard to "Mulder and Scully" by Catatonia.

Then there was the time during one of our *soirees* when the boys and I bit the heads off a few bats we found in the garage, and we spat the heads at these Hot Topic cunts.

"What's the Frequency, Kenneth?" by R.E.M. was playing when Savage's pantleg of his red skeleton jumpsuit somehow caught on fire and that chick he was fucking at the time—I think her name was Hope or something (can't remember)—she's a photographer and brilliantly captured a fantastic photo of him thrashing around. And I still think we should use that picture for our next album cover.

What *next* fucking album? That's the problem with raging all the time: we are not making any new music. Which is odd because the *booze* has always been my *muse*.

"In 'n' Out of Grace" by Mudhoney played when we fought those fucking *Oi!* assholes from New Haven who started throwing fists in the mosh pit. Cunts. That may have been back in winter actually. Like I said, these romps blend together. It's almost as if this year has been one BIG party.

Erik threw an empty beer bottle at that old bitch's face that time. Savage was shitting blood, squatting over a storm drain.

"Tortured Souls" is the thirteenth track from disc 0 of Painkiller's four-disc box set titled *Painkiller: The Collected Works*. We smoke unfiltered cigarettes as we listen to John Zorn's magic saxophone while we take turns using the garden hose to bathe in the driveway.

I think it was around Easter when we noticed that dead guy in the car parked in front of the house next door. We told the piggies we didn't recognize him. Then after they threw him in the bag to bring him to the pauper's grave or wherever, an officer turned the car on and Skin Yard's "Nietzsche with a Pizza" started blaring, and we laughed and said he was probably a guest at our last shindig.

We held chainsaw dancing competitions like Leatherface at the end of *The Texas Chainsaw Massacre*. I think that was our New Year's party! I remember because Erik made a big deal about the wolf moon.

PART 1

FIRST CHAPTER

July 28, 1999
Backyard, evening

"Although the sun is at all times above the earth's surface, it appears in the morning to ascend from the northeast to the noonday position, and thence to descend and disappear, or set, in the northwest. This phenomenon arises from the operation of a simple and everywhere visible law of perspective."

"New book?" I ask, somewhat rhetorically if not flat-out sarcastic.

Erik is reading aloud chapter 9, "Cause of Sunrise and Sunset," from a book titled *Zetetic Astronomy: Earth Not a Globe* by Samuel Birley Rowbotham.

"This book was written in the nineteenth century, and it is a simple, easy-to-follow guide on understanding the true shape of our planet. It is not a globe, sir!"

"Oh boy!" I sense another personality shift a-coming!

"No, it is not. It is flat. There are illustrations."

I spark a cigarette. "Are you doing some sort of bit right now? Is this comedy hour in Erik's world?"

"We are going to use this! This is going right into our mythos," Erik says, tossing the book onto the backyard picnic table that is positioned slightly behind him. "What do you think?"

"I think we will get sued if we keep trying to incorporate all these books you are reading into our stage presence. I'm sure they copywrote—wait, is it copywritten or copyrighted?"

Erik makes the same kind of smirk a mother would make at their fucking toddler trying to say words. "*Copyrighted* is past tense for *copyright*."

We are sitting in lawn chairs in the backyard, enjoying the day's waning light while in the comfortable shade of the poisonous pear tree.

Savage asks, "How hot was it today?" He—quite pensively, I might add—is writing something down.

"Not as hot as Rome," Erik says as he applies a little A+D ointment to the new tattoo over his abs. It reads: *Hungry man, reach for the book; it is a weapon.* "Christ. Do you hear me? Low 90s. Anything in the 90s or above is technically heat wave status."

Savage says, "But since our little bouts last week."

Erik snorts.

Savage continues, "Since our little bouts! Of-of-of fucking dehydration last week."

Erik erupts. "I almost died! And I'm still pissing little chunks of brown mucus."

Savage screams, "I FUCKING TOLD YOU TO DRINK THE PEDIALYTE! Did—wait. Did you say 'brown mucus'?" Savage sits, looks at me. "That's a good name." Then he goes back to writing in his little pad of legal yellow paper.

Band names or the next new name. That special one that inspires it all—it's our shop talk. Band names, venue names, sociopathic lyrics. This is our new language: The Guttersnipes, Pussy Secretions, Set Your Dogs on Fire, Set Your Mom on Fire, We Fuck Fire, Jerkoff Firefighters, Fuck Firefighters, and now the present Fuck'd for Life.

This band—the effort and momentum, both individually and when harnessed as teamwork—has the potential for…what? We are becoming some survivor organism addicted to adapting, evolving, and being increasingly procedural with our nonverbal communication. Something minute, transmitted and received in a fraction of a second—twenty-first century.

Savage says, "We are becoming a hydra." And I know he is feeling good, all acidic and shit. You can see this drug swimming in someone's eyes.

Erik snatches the picture I've been working on: a new theme.

He holds the picture out to Savage, and how he does it—the deliberate, slow, thought-out action he employs—I know he is feeling something. Not to mention, I chuckle loudly when I notice this. Erik's eyes are welling up, and his black holes are fucking crazy big. "Cerberus," he says, showing my drawing of the mythological three-headed wild dog giant that guards the gates of the underworld.

The effects of the acid are now being felt. The anatomy of a trip. Trip for the work and a-MUSE-ment. My stomach is a theatre of ominous synth music. My eyes: distortion.

Savage says, "Holy moly." A moment later, he lies on the grass, and I see the grass give under his mass and volume. I see now, in that instant, grass as a whole organism. One mind.

My brain is the producer, the mixer, the man in the booth, or the one that holds our leash. They're giving the feed at a higher tempo and diminishing the logical faculties of my brain.

There's a slight pulse to everything that I know to be, in my heart of hearts, the universe waving hello.

This is lysergic acid diethylamide, waving you hello. Erik is crunch-activating his palmful of glow sticks, neon spaghetti. He throws or rather fucking heaves them up into the air to ungroup and disperse, land cushion-quiet, speckling soft green in the living darkness.

My cock and balls—*our* cock and balls. We are punk rock, so hopefully, this is the soul of our music, in your face. That's right. Our cock and balls are in and around your face—so close you can smell it. Go ahead, smell it. SMELL OUR BALLS.

"Guys, we really need to push the fucking envelope here. We need to rebrand!"

My heart pounds like the frenzy of Savage's drumming. I can feel it brimming throughout my leg blood, my neck, beckoning me to go outside. I am outside. *No. Go out farther.*

Yup, this is starting to feel just like the last time. Erik and Savage howl at the moon. It is a full moon tonight—*more specifically, a buck moon.*

July 28, 1999 (23:12)

"Werewolves of London" by Warren Zevon plays.

Savage says, "We should play some Bush."

Erik scoffs, "Just play with yours! I vote NO. It was freakin' bad enough seeing him at Woodstock. No wonder Rome fell." Erik says this as he tosses his book on the picnic table. A new one.

"Done with the book on not eating? Done with the flat-Earth book? What about the new tattoo? Can you focus on one BREAK-THROUGH life philosophy at a time?"

Erik uses the opportunity to flash us his abs again. "The moral answerability I extracted from Mr. Sinclair's work, the essence, has been distilled, and a commitment has been made. The tattoo is a symbol."

"I don't get it, Erik. What's the meaning?" I put a silly emphasis to this word when I ask it as I am a professional asshole and avid hobbyist. "Is it herbal?"

Erik smiles and I get a bad feeling. I knew all his reading was going to fuck him up—even more than he already was. That's an important distinction to make. He was always a bad dog. I should save him from the overwhelming effect of wisdom and burn the remaining unopened packages, throw them right into the firepit.

Savage rolls in the grass giggling, having fun, talking to someone clearly more fun than Erik right now.

Erik laughs, and for a split second, the moon dually reflects in his black shades. "Hunger." He says this entirely straight-faced; he's not fucking joking. "The secret to life, to the power of it, has always been being hungry." He slides his new book over to me: *White Fang* by Jack London. "Hunger keeps you eager. Driven. Horny. And that is equivalent to rage, and that drive is what yields all-meaning success."

"Equivalent for you maybe." *Don't get frustrated*, I tell myself. "Are you fucking tripping, Erik? 'Cause I am not feeling a thing."

He points to the moon, and suddenly, there it is. The shift. A carnival ride jolting its creaking parts before the full momentum of the mechanics come to life, and you start up the coaster's initial incline. Take note, kids. Let the trip come to you.

Then the ride drops.

I vomit first. This, in turn, activates Savage's gastrological empathy. And when he boots, he sounds like he is playing a tuba filled with mud. We hear animals scurry out of the trees and bushes, and I see that one of the streetlights to the front flickers rapidly, then dies out.

And it is like the moon, or our reverence of it, that activates these new weird doings of night play. Doesn't growth occur at night—plants and children and fingernails and such? Nocturnally photosynthetic, we eat moonshine. That should be the name of our next album.

Savage jumps on the picnic table when the fire dies out. We play "Celebration of the Lizard King" by Jim Morrison as he throws his shithouse frame through the pressure-treated wood, and it cracks and splinters off in medium-length chunks like pyrate cutlasses.

"That was my grandfather's," I say.

"Fuck your grandfather."

"Fuck your mother."

"Her too."

"Cunt."

Savage says, "Breaking shit. Doesn't really pair with butter. I mean, yes, I can break stuff. And yes, I am good at breaking stuff. But if I am being honest, my heart wasn't in it just now with the picnic table, and I feel you guys could sense that."

That's what we are calling acid now: butter. And we don't say "drop acid" anymore. We say "pop" as in "let's pop tonight and moon-worship." This has a double meaning for us because we also use that as code for partying like Keith Moon, the late drummer for the Who and a legendary rock and roll drunken madman. This is all particular to our rock and roll patois.

If I ever wrote a love story, it would be about alcohol and how consuming large amounts numbs the incidental pain and bullshit that festers in my soul so I can take my music to the next goddamn level.

Savage says, "I am really responding to the fire though, and it looks like you guys are too. BURNING SHIT is better with butter!" We're in boxers now, and he points out our erections, goddammit. I jokingly yell "cut!" like we are on a movie set, and it gets a laugh.

We shiver: "acidic jitters." We exchange a-ha looks and clever smirking; this happens in fuck-all of a second. And there it is, a simple display of our collectivity, what equals to synchronicity and time and a cunt-fart of magic that comes when each individual part works together. Isn't music, the band—isn't that the shining example of what teamwork means? Harmony.

Got to meet the muse halfway, right?

Here's some other shit that happened that night (probably):

1. *Erik has headphones on, and he's singing along to "Mr. Roboto" by Styx. "I've never heard this song like this before. Holy frickin' crap!" He's taking off his clothes and saying he needs a rock and roll makeover.*

2. *Classic Nick puts on a plaid onesie and puts on the Spencer David Group. The song "I'm a Man" plays, and with a razor blade, he starts cutting the glow sticks and throwing the neon fluid* EVERYWHERE.

3. *Someone puts in the album* Meet the Residents *from the Residents. The song "Breath and Length" plays when the boys have a ninja fight using the plastic glow-in-the-dark stars intended for a child's ceiling. The secret is to "charge them up" with the black lights first, and when you throw them, they dissolve into darkness, just like real shooting stars.*

4. *Johnny Menthol, the neighbor from next door, makes a brief cameo appearance. He reveals himself suddenly and dramatically. He fashions nunchucks out of glow sticks, and he's showing off his hand-eye coordination, not to mention his unique Latin flair when it comes to* TWIRLING. *That's what the boys*

will start calling it. The LSD-fueled expression your entire mortal being exerts when blasted with those sweet and sexy tunes. Your body knows it when it's there. And it is sexy. It's very sexy. Mr. Menthol's nunchucks here, they are dissolved of violence. It's all heart and soul and pathos and magic utilized here at the Red House. We're chock-full of magic.

5. *Erik shows off his new rock and roll look. He calls it power-clashing: leopard print tights and a Hawaiian shirt. He says, "This is just the beginning. You see, I have (stole!) this Yes/No coin engraved with all sorts of kind of trippy, kind of demonic iconography. I find a piece of apparel that catches my eye, I leave it to the gods to decide. I flip. The eyeballs in the palm of the hand side says Yes, I add it. If No, I get the winged skeleton demon. The gods speak through human games of chance and reward the few mortals that relinquish their will to the* HIGHER FORCES. *Why do you think I suggested we play Russian roulette for our last show?"*

6. *Savage puts on Prince, his all-time favorite musician, and the song "1999" comes on. There's a knock on the front door, and the Mt. Holyoke girls are here. They are into the rough stuff, notoriously. They have a duffel bag with them, and they say they brought toys to play with. They say this smiling while the frontwoman—a tall babe that goes by English Black Dahlia—*TWIRLS *a pair of handcuffs on her index finger. She's biting her lip.*

7. *They order takeout that no one will eat. And when the delivery guy shows up, Erik pops out from the basement window and tells him he's been held captive. That he's a prisoner.*

   "Don't listen to him!" Savage shouts down from the low-pitched rooftop. "Just hand me the food."

   "No," Erik says. "I'm the rightful owner. Give it to me."

   "He's just an abject basement guy, kind pizza man. Pay no mind! He's rubbish. In fact, go ahead and pull your cock out and pee on his face a bit. Go on!"

Erik shouts, "Don't do it, brother. It's not worth it. But feel free to throw a turd up at him or something. Or better yet—spit. Can you spit that far?"

Erik and Savage erupt into hysterics.

Classic Nick comes out the front door. He's wearing his Black Flag baseball hat, and the ball-gag in his mouth is loosened and resting around his neck, and that's all. "Don't listen to these acidheads, pizza man," he says, wearing peach lipstick. He gives the guy a twenty. "They're freaks." And he blows him a kiss.

8. *Erik, now in his bedroom, tells English Black Dahlia—who's by far the hottest of the Mt. Holyoke girls—that he prefers to make whoopee with Frank Zappa playing in the background.*

She says through the bathroom door, "That's fine, my little Moon Unit."

Erik puts on the album Uncle Meat. *He hits shuffle, and the track "Nine Types of Industrial Pollution" comes on.*

English Black Dahlia steps out bare-assed, save for a life-like apparatus.

"What the hell is that?"

"It's a silicone penis attached to my pelvic area, courtesy of this four-strap harness. I only have Caucasian flavor, so consider yourself spared."

"A strap-on dildo. I suppose that big vein bulging out the side of it is integral to its function?"

She laughs. "That's right. You did say you're down for anything. Or are you a pussy now that you're away from your boyfriends?"

"One moment," Erik says while he fishes through his jeans to find the Yes/No coin.

9. *The mushrooms are called Penis Envy. Classic Nick takes his as tea. That's his preferred method of taking them. Chop them up (dicing or what have you), put them in a cup, and add hot water. "It tastes like shit," he says. "But you sip on it casually. Sip by sip and trip by trip."*

Erik just downs his. One big bite. He chases it with orange juice after because he says vitamin C really punches up the psilocybin.

Savage says he wants to infuse his with alcohol and channel his spirit animal like a Viking berserker. He doesn't, of course. His spirit animal is probably a gorilla or extinct hominid of some kind. No, he just takes his share of the stems and caps and eats them like the fucking Holy Eucharist or something. "It tastes like shit, but they get the job done." The boys think doing magic mushrooms at the end of an acid trip is called hippie-flipping—it's not.

10. *Outside, there is howling in some direction, maybe a block away. The boys immediately think of that book* White Fang *and howl back.*

Savage says, "I think the moon is howling tonight."

11. *The boys, in a blitzkrieg state of derealization, are swigging dark beers whilst watching* Bad Lieutenant *and tattooing poor facsimiles of the "parental advisory" warning on themselves, sporadically playing songs over the muted audio of the movie. Songs like "Drug Store" by the Dwarves and "Don't Fear the Reaper" by Gus.*

Before they crash and just as the sun is coming up, the boys and the Mt. Holyoke girls go out to the backyard. The boys are naked. The Mt. Holyoke girls are wearing the boys' Bruins jerseys with the new bear head logo, personalized with their last names. They laugh and scream and drink and laugh some more.

This is not your life. They are heightened. This is life when you embrace the chaos and fire and flesh that comes with rock and roll. This is not your life.

Here is some advice. Take drugs and turn up the volume, and maybe you too will expose a little truth as sacred clowns sometimes do because this is definitely not your life.

Second Chapter

August 7, 1999

Today, let's just make a quick acknowledgment to the Blizzard River accident at Six Flags New England that happened earlier, as in today. One dead and, I believe, like eleven injured or some such shit. And now, because of our rock and rolling, on this date and the significance of all that encumbers, those Blizzard River folks and, to a lesser extent, their families (kind of), they have become *absorbed* into OUR story, where their historicity and all that symbolizes will be processed and broken down like the building blocks of all our booze and drugs and monkeyshines and then redistributed into the LIFEBLOOD of our band of pyrates. Our tale: the pyrate-tail.

August 13, 1999 (23:00)

Today, for what little remains of it, is Friday the thirteenth, so me and the boys earlier watched Jason in *Friday the 13th Part 2*, which I say is the best one because it's before the hockey mask, and he just has a one-holed sack over his head. But Erik says part 4 with the guy who's pretending he's Jason is better, but then a few minutes later, Savage says that *Jason Goes to Hell* is the best, and we toast our tequilas.

We're also on about twelve hits of acid each. Just us alone, chilling. Just me and the boys.

August 20, 1999

I like my girlfriends, and I really hesitate to use that fucking word, to have some sort of damnation edge to them, you follow? Similar to me in the sense that I am a bad news bear. Going to hell and the like. God's only reprobate where, fifty years from now, posters of my mug shots will be hanging on the dorm walls of budding young degenerates who, like ourselves, hear the call of Black Bell of the underworld, which isn't a real thing. At least, I don't think it is but definitely something we can work into our band mythos.

"Your main bitch," Erik says covertly, careful not to hip English Black Dahlia, who is in the other room, to his rude, crude jargon. "Instead of girlfriend."

"My *Maine* bitch?"

He gives what I value as a perfunctory grin. "Yeah. Your main bitch. What's the trouble?"

Maybe he recently nabbed a Stephen King book or something? I really don't know about him sometimes. I take my mason jar and my bottle of tequila, and we join Savage and the ladies in the basement, which in the past *whatever* days since our last trip, Savage has been diligently and secretly remodeling according to a vision or a dream or whatever he said. Granted, I try to please my muse too, of course, but she's got Savage buying sheets of frickin' fabrics and a whole lotta other crap. Sorry, Charlie, but not my muse. No thanks.

The basement is semifinished. A lot of wood paneling. This was there since we took over the place.

Savage says, "It's not art, but I like it."

He is referring to the basement *now* as I broodingly trod down into it.

And more than him that likes it, there's Erik and English Black Dahlia and Becca and Tatiana and…yeah. Now there's comfortable seating in the form of a charcoal(?) sectional and (gulp!) some shag carpeting under that sectional. Oh yeah. And the shag carpeting is, for whatever reason, white. But what the hell do I care? Let's have some fun. And there's also some erratic lighting choices with Xmas lights: orange and red and blue and white strands braided together forming what, symbolically, I guess is the colour palette for fire. I surely don't know.

My *Coors Light* mirror is on the wall. I ask Savage if he properly secured it because it's bad luck if you break a mirror.

Becca and Tatiana belong to me and Savage, respectively. I don't know statuses right, mine or Savage's. But like I said, I don't need status as much as I dig a more fluid type thing, although Savage and Totty—brackets and then the word SIC—seem to be hitting it off. And of course, there's salt and pepper here that are riding the highway through the danger zone.

"The word is a compound word. Richard Lederer, in his book *Crazy English* that came out last year, he said the culmination of these words: super- ("above"), cali- ("beauty"), fragilistic- ("delicate"), expiali- ("to atone"), and -docious ("educable"). Then when COMPOUNDED—"

Erik cuts her off. "Which means!" He is noticeably excited. "Meeting you, like I said, has been supercalifragilisticexpialidocious."

They giggle (or share a giggle, you could say), and who knew Erik was a giggler? Still, part of me thinks his inner son of a bitch ain't going nowhere. They kiss and that act goes around the room like a yawn or the rippling wave in a stadium. And while all this *necking* occurs, I open my eyes to then notice the crucifixes on the wall. But they are covered in paint, or what I suspect as paint could also be elementary school white glue. Ya know, that tasty shit. Savage could have doused these crucifixes, the entire dozen or so. But there's probably an odd number, knowing Savage, so like eleven or thirteen crucifixes covered in thick globs of white. But he applied the gunk with them upside down so when they are turned over properly like the good Lord intended, the thick drool lines aim toward the sky, and it's creepy. Like zero-gravity creepy, except it looks like someone jizzed all over these weird statues of tortured messiahs, and this causes shit to aim toward heaven like it's the end of the world and all his followers are being called home. I shiver.

Savage says, "At the end of days, our physical world will be left for the hyenas." And he blasts a backlight, and cum-glue hard-dried on all these little Jesus H. Christs start to GLOW.

"No wolves," Erik interjects.

And English Black Dahlia nods approvingly, adding, "They are an APEX PREDATOR." And another kiss works its way through the room, and I hear "Right Here, Right Now" by Jesus Jones playing softly on a radio left on upstairs.

Erik fumbles a new book from within the couch. There's a wolf on the cover, and it looks like a real cheap cover, and he wants talk about this new book now. I know it, gawd damn it.

"Hyenas are scavengers. Rebecca agrees," I say, gesturing to the contented look on her face. "And the end of the world, yeah. It implies that God only took what was salvageable and LEFT THE REST FOR THE BEASTS."

Totty says, "And their"—she does air quotes—"'laughter' could most certainly be interpreted as DEMONIC."

I called her Rebecca and she didn't correct me, as I assume her preference is what she was introduced as. That's interesting. I am suddenly curious if she introduced herself to me or someone else introduced her. I'm thinking in terms of cause and effect, name given versus name got. Regardless, I was probably drunk on tequila because as of this summer, Summer of '99, I am a tequila boy. Not to mention Woodstock '99, which put us on the path of TWIRLING.

We pop the E/X/Ecstasy. We do it in unions, and we cheer our doublestacks, and we are in a circle in Savage's basement betwixt the reach of the portioned couch that "I am now realizing it is dark red, like liver blood."

Charcoal blood?

Tatiana says, interjecting, says, "Dark red because it's carrying carbon dioxide. Oxygenated blood is your classic bright red." Totty pauses to giggle. And there it is, another fucking giggler in the house. So talk about shit that will drive you to drink.

Erik asks for a sip of my tequila. Then Savage needs a hit, and this jar o' mine of Summer of '99 is passed around real Keith-Moon quick while Totty covers her mouth 'cause this chick is laughing so hard. I ask Savage if she's already feeling the effects, and he answers that she's bullshit or silly or green or whatever. He does this by giving a slow shrug, continuing like we rehearsed this. English Black Dahlia throws one back and shivers. I then give it to Becca, but she doesn't shiver, so that's cool.

Totty says, "I can already tell this is good shit. Where did you get this from?"

"Woodstock '99," I say. Then I finish the finger or two of tequila left in my mason jar. Then fast like a Band-Aid, I *pat* Becca on the leg or, even bolder, *slide my hand* on her lower back—slide smoothly like a runner stealing second. And so that's the motion I go with to ask her if she wants to join me in doing something fun with tequila, and she nods yes.

Savage says, "I am going to let this one supply the tunes." And he is obviously talking about Totty.

"Are we sure this is better than outside by the fire?" I ask in a "show mercy on me" tone, and again, Savage shrugs. And I think, *What the hell does that mean?* Then English Black Dahlia asks Erik if he wants to drink her urine, and he is chuckling up those stairs speedily in a fucking daaaaaaassssssssssh, and she's coming up the rear of him. Gawd damn. That's a choice of words, huh?

I smile to myself as, once again, I grab the tequila bottle, and up the stairs we go. And all the while, I stare at her. What is she, Latina or part? Because, Christ-of-prayers, I am staring at the thick fluctuations heaving in her plump-dumper, gawd damn bell-bottoms, and it is sexy and sensual and stimulating because I start to feel my mushroom swell and pulsate hot with my dick-blood.

And without realizing it, Classic Nick suddenly stiff in his jaw muscles and seeping to his other muscles, in response to the brown booty in those bell-bottoms, his pupils dilate, and his I WANT *muscles correspond accordingly to his biology, now with the psychoactive MDMA pooling like the liquid chemiluminescence in glow sticks around the gray sponge in his head.*

Classic Nick thinks as he jostles the bottle up the stairs, taking big whiffs and coming up the rear, as it were, Well, at least she's on her period tonight.

August 20, 1999

Emerging from the basement, I am licking my chops.

It's called rolling because you are in motion like the undulating juice in Becca's booty roasts. Prime-cut butcher's special and fresh like the blood falling down my chin—oh so juicy. The dribbles. Hot sticky kisses that fill the bulbous anteroom of my nose with that metallic tinge even though I am choosing not to actively take in the balmy scent. Then coming from downstairs, "Smack My Bitch Up" by the Prodigy starts up, and I quickly wonder if that is Totty's choice or what. I hack like a cat, and you never know if you get it or there's now an everlasting tickle you are very much going to have to get used to.

I uncouple from the burgundy gash, her plump sausage thighs and fertile hips that demand it all. My coming up for air made a tiny suction sound like it's soup I'm slurping through. I hack again, and I think the hair is still there. I look up at Becca's dilated eyes.

*****

After anal sex, Totty mentions how she likes new music. Anything right now and happening is her favorite song, and that's that.

"I can work with that," Savage replies candidly and hops up the basement stairs to the black-market tapes in his room from his whatever Greek or something contact in Worchester that hooks him up with boot-leg early releases. He opens the door to find Becca bent over the kitchen counter and Classic Nick's face planted right in it. Sucking bloody cunt. Classic Nick comes back to the world, passion-eyed and feeling refreshed. He looks at Savage with his redwings real and slick, then motions, asking for a cigarette.

Then he looks up at her, all watery eyed on the counter. "You want a cigarette, Becca?"

*****

Savage says, "Maybe in the morning, we can do Ritalin and watch *Cat People* again?"

Totty responds with "Don't you guys need to play shows on the weekend?" And at this, we laugh and high-five and toast our tequilas. Dumb fucking bitch.

"Call this our refractory period," Erik says as we all make our way to the backyard. "Anyway, Class needs to seduce his muse with fire and anarchy."

"Like real bastard pyrates."

On the ghetto blaster, Savage plays "Cat People (Putting Out Fire)" by David Bowie, and I ignite the firepit with rubber cement and a road flare, and it's like we're suddenly back at Woodstock. Everyone cheers as the flames lick toward the moon, and we howl real frickin' bestial howls that emanate DEEP from within our center masses.

Rebecca and English Black Dahlia brought handfuls of glow sticks and those plastic connectors, thank the fuck Christ. Now all the ingredients are present, and we can really party.

22:22

I read my friend Jamie's suicide note to the girls. I read it over a synth remix of "O Fortuna," and this makes Rebecca sob, and Totty tells me to stop. Savage plays "Love Is the Drug" by Roxie Music. I still have the blood on my mouth like a nasty clown smile. I tell Savage to turn up the heat, and he takes a mouthful of gasoline and spits it on the fire. English Black Dahlia asks me if the suicide note is real. I tell her that he hung himself from a tree along the river near the Basketball Hall of Fame.

"What was he running from?"

I make my hands like I'm a priest giving a sermon. "Isn't it obvious?" I'm referring to the millennium, and she nods solemnly and quietly realizes I'm referring to the millennium.

Erik makes a chain of glow sticks that he begins to TWIRL in front of a bush he set on fire, and I tell everyone to pay attention. "Erik is telling a story." And we revere the spectacle because a burning bush means God has just arrived at the party, and if we are heightened enough to hear his voice, it would officially mean we are the doomsday prophets chosen to witness the end of the world.

"According to Dante's *The Inferno*," English Black Dahlia says, "all suicides spend eternity in hell as trees that can only speak if their branches or bark are painfully ripped off because, for people that kill themselves, they can only communicate through suffering."

I laugh and throw another log onto the fire. Erik stops TWIRL-ING and tells her that we cut his suicide-tree down weeks ago, and that's the wood we are currently burning, and her eyes get big and incredulous. At the same time, some sap or something pops within the blaze, sending a comet of sparks. "I think Jamie just said hello."

Savage plays "Beat's So Lonely" by Charlie Sexton. I tell the girls this song is featured rather epically in the classic '80s teen romance *Some Kind of Wonderful*.

I tell English Black Dahlia to slap Erik's face. She does. Then I tell her she must do it twice. She smiles and gives him another one. We laugh.

Savage says that Elias Koteas's character, Duncan, is his spirit animal, and he lives to fuck with yuppies.

"You BOYS are absolutely mental."

Erik points up at the tree line. "Bats operate under the agency of the head vampires." He pulls out his cock and pisses out the bush fire. "This celebration no longer has a place for God."

Totty says, "How do you know that was the tree your friend hung himself on?"

I go to the garage and come back with a short cut of an old tattered rope.

Rebecca gasps. "No way. That can't be the same rope."

I smirk my bloody grin, then dip the frayed end into the embers.

"What are you doing!"

I tell Savage to kill the vibe, and he plays "Rope on Fire" by Morphine.

The boys get their glow stick chains and position themselves behind me as my backup dancers, and then we begin to TWIRL, giving the ladies a private show, showcasing TRUE synchronicity of our chemical madness.

After, Rebecca requests a song, and Savage tells her this isn't TRL. Totty tells him to play nice. He huffs and when she tells him the song, he laughs and says, "That's actually a great choice." He digs for the cassette and then, after a minute, plays "Moving in Stereo" by the Cars.

And then the girls join in, and together, we begin to TWIRL around the fire.

Next Chapter

August 26, 1999 (23:23)

Then smash cut and it's almost a week later, and here we are again, throwing back more doublestacks because too much, too soon is the nature of the beast, and we all want to get our kicks before this shithouse goes up in flames. Dead Jamie did say in his suicide note that bad times were coming, but tonight, I read my friend Steve the Rapper's letter from prison. In it, he tells me he is going to kill himself.

"You're running out of time because bad times are coming..."

As for suicide notes, I think it sucked ass, so no joke. I grade the paper with a big F on the top of the first page. In red magic.

Savage is playing some of his bootlegs for Totty. He puts on a new one. He says, "This one is 'Hey Joe' by Make-Up, and this won't be out till autumn."

For instance, today was the first time I cummed in Rebecca, and I do not mean her pussy. Then as we were getting our clothes back on, she tells me that sexual fetishizing of the butt is called *pygophilia*. I think, *Gawd dammit. Don't you fall for this broad, Class. Do not contract the monogamy virus.*

The boys and I make everyone mixed drinks of mostly tequila and Pedialyte. "It's important to stay hydrated," I say as I hand out the red solo cups.

"William Blake said 'the road of excess leads to the palace of wisdom.'" English Black Dahlia says this as she takes her X with a gulp of tequila. "You think your friend the rapist will actually kill himself, or is it all talk?"

Totty says cheers and extends her cup. "Nothing exceeds like excess." And her face puckers when her tongue touches the tequila. Then she shivers. She's silhouetted before the flames.

"He's tried to in the past," I say to English Black Dahlia. "And that sounds gay, but he was serious every time."

"Every time?"

"Both times," I correct myself. "But I'll swear to Lizard King he definitely tried to kill himself. It just didn't take. And not only that, but also his letters to me both times we're fucking amazing." Then I signal her *one moment*, and I nudge Rebecca to drink up. "It's important we all make this plunge together."

"Plunge is right," she says. "I feel I'm about to cannonball into the DEEP END. I'm not typically this free-spirited. I think you may soon find how boring I actually am."

"Just go with it. Don't fight it. You might surprise yourself."

Rebecca cheers her red solo with Totty and she with English Black Dahlia and back to Becca as they say.

*****

And when she starts sipping, the boys, share an exchange of quick looks and even quicker smiles. Blink and you might miss it. If this were a movie, this would be the perfect time for a break of the fourth wall because what the girls don't know is that the boys added about six drops of lysergic acid diethylamide to each of the red solo cups. These boys are such jerks, they should be cartoon characters drawn with stink lines, bratty-boy attributes, and frequently depicted pooing on things or ideas the common woman or man holds in high esteem. MDMA and LSD, when done together, is called candyflipping. Summer of '99 is about taking it to the next level, so raise the black flag and navigate these tumultuous seas like a bastard pyrate with a declaration of war against reality.

*****

Savage plays a song called "Bloodsucker" by Paralysed Age. He says, "Again, not officially out till autumn."

"Nature of the beast," I say as we say cheers before the raging firepit.

"Goodness." Rebecca lowers the cup from her lips. "You certainly look like a BEAST. You still have my *punctuation* all over your face." She says this and, like the mother of a small child, licks her finger and tries wiping away my burgundy grin.

I evade her hand. "Leave it," I say. "Play bloody games, win bloody prizes."

Savage says, "That's it for the unreleased stuff for today, Totty. Gotta make what I have last, unfortunately, as I just learned that my Worcester connection just joined a Y2K cult that prohibits the use of any technology developed after 1899. I wished him well. After I read their blog and they seem…*passionate*. But, boy, I hope they let him keep his hearing aids."

Rebecca earlier today told me she has a condition called menorrhagia, which means for ten days a month, she bleeds like a slasher movie. So indeed, today I praise the blessed name of Lucifer, for this is nothing less than a bloody miracle. Over jeans, I put my hand between her legs, delighting in the extra heat of what Rebecca remarked wasn't a *period* but, rather, an *exclamation point*.

I add, "At least, this time, I remembered to say my prayers before feasting."

And when I say this, she flashes me a wild look like "Oh shit. I am really falling hard for this madman-rocker blood-pervert punk-pyrate trip junkie." I could also be overreading things. Who the fuck knows? She is, after all, on a few drugs.

Savage plays "Mouth (The Stingray Mix)" by Bush. Then Totty points to the trees. "Wind is starting to pick up."

Erik, like a schizoid, points up to the sky. "Waxing crescent moon." He says this to no one in particular, and after highlighting this point, he returns to his lawn chair and resumes reading from his black book with the bipedal wolf on it. I can see the title now: *The Book of Werewolves: Being an Account of Terrible Superstition* by Sabine Baring-Gould.

"Read me something, babe," English Black Dahlia says, putting her arm around him and laying the side of her head on his shoulder.

"I love when you read to me." She runs her hand over the many homemade tattoos on his arm, courtesy of me mostly.

Savage says, "I thought this was a party." He throws a glow stick at him. "Erik! What the fuck are you doing, man? Let's party."

Erik flicks his cigarette, which nails Savage square in the forehead. He shouts, "I told you before. Fuck Bush. Fuck post-grunge! I expressed my disinterest many times over. So now when you play it, I am going to check out and read my books." He takes a sip/gulp/chug from the red solo, then adds, "Gavin Rossdale gave me bad vibes at Woodstock."

English Black Dahlia tries tickling Erik. "Babe, c'mon. Try to be human tonight."

Savage doesn't say anything—at least, not about Bush. Instead, he waits maybe a half minute, all the while matching Erik in mouthfuls from the red solo. And then after a short period of fumbling through cassettes, Savage changes the song to "Because the Night" by Patti Smith, and when this happens, Totty screeches with excitement.

Rebecca gives a quick clap, like she's giving an abridged applause. "My song!"

"Erik fucking Worthley, interact with your fucking sexy girlfriend," English Black Dahlia says, shooting him grim glances like she's harboring sheer hate but coyly takes his hand and guides it to her crotch. She smiles and bites her lip. Clearly, she's already feeling something while pale and dead-eyed Erik looks like he's imploding.

*****

Erik, until a few hours prior, was spending his Thursday getting what he calls "weird drunk," a common enough occurrence where he adds a "sick dose" of cough syrup with codeine to his lemonade and sparkling wine, which he drinks from an actual chalice he stole from a Catholic priest. And he'll drink twelve chalices of this transformative elixir at a time, no shit. He gets what the boys described as "fey." His emotions become all over the place, and he'll cry-laugh and recount all sorts of weird episodes from his life, like how when he was thirteen and a mall Santa with Down syndrome cornered him in the back of the arcade and asked him to hold on to an organ transport cooler until "the coast was clear."

Being weird drunk also makes him, for whatever reason, break into city hall, the post office, and other municipal buildings to "let his hair down" and camp out for the night. And one time, he was hit by a car twice in one day! He's also given long detailed confessions to famous crimes that would have been impossible for him to commit. These confessions always involve the most peculiar and random motives that make no sense, like being the Boston Strangler "for the money" or killing JonBenét Ramsey "to promote Esperanto as our national language." Springfield and a few other local Massachusetts police departments have active restraining orders on him, and his 1997 interview with Players—*a soft-core porno magazine that was commonly referred to as "the black Playboy"—has, to this day, never been published.*

August 27, 1999 (00:33)

Candyflipping, field tripping, and listening to Type O Negative.

Savage is driving. We take the Blunderbus, and now we all agree just to nix the tequila. The girls are drinking pickle juice and seltzer with lemon juice—all three ingredients they somehow found in the house. I don't know how old that shit is. Oh lawdy. That's surely a sin because me and the boys are drinking delicious cold Pedialyte for hydration because, as English Black Dahlia said, we are mushroom-clouding through this trip. Rolling trip. Our NONSTOP pop rock and *rolling* trip.

And good for us for getting out of the house. We flipped on it, but the girls said they'll come along, but no open booze while we are out, and we had to pinky-swear to that end! And I reiterated this several times, that we really don't want to drink now because—personally, and I haven't verbally made this out there yet naturally—but I think this may be a bad trip.

Erik for sure. He is drowning in a personal piss river, it looks like, and maybe I'm just feeding off his vibes. He's not saying nothing now after reading about LYCANTHROPY, just sitting there sweaty on the bus seat meant for retarded schoolchildren or sometimes sticking his head out the window to vomit. Makes me vomit.

Rebecca said that's because I am deeply empathetic, which I think sounds like she's calling me gay. But she laughed hard when I said that, so I'll just accept her words at face value.

"Lycan-THROPY," I say aloud, but saying it kind of like I'm saying "throw-upy." Rebecca's curious about this one, no laugh. Shitty. I shrug-smile. "Fun word."

"He ate the page after he read from it," she quickly says.

I snap my fingers! Aha! I forgot he did that. "That's why he threw up. Erik's stomach gets wonky when he eats paper."

"In our little tribe here that we call a band, we value weird and bold actions that echo loud throughout the empty halls of the everyday humdrum."

"You're a poet, Nicholas," she says even quicker. It just hangs in the air.

"Whoa."

"You've got quite the SILVER tongue is what I'm saying."

"You called me Nicholas." I find myself looking around when I say this, like I'm nervous, whispering it like it's a bad word.

"That's your actual name, isn't it?"

It isn't. Classic Nick is his legal designation.

We head downtown to where the city's tall buildings stand. We want lights. We crave neon. There's something special about us now—right now. A truth maybe. The Muse. We need to be around humans and all their inner functions. I want to see them sweat and breathe. We must join them where they play their night games, see what darkness makes of them. How they entertain their shadows is a direct result in how we live life after dusk.

Humans are pure darkness on the inside, and that's what we can share. They need to witness our magics firsthand. We must show them the moon—the real moon—and how its shine changes our colours. Red to black and so forth, for blood flows in its natural state to the scenery of black waters. Our task is to teach them. To play missionary and show the unconverted how to exist within colours and darkness. And when these concepts exist IN STEREO, the moonlight becomes the only fuel you need or will ever need. We must show them the menacing size of our dilated pupils. We will show them that consuming only moonlight is the only real way you can combat reality.

A gang of dirt bikers (maybe six) pass us on the right and kick and punch the side of the Blunderbus as Savage sails us down Union Street. Totty and English Black Dahlia pop their heads out of the windows and laugh at their antics. Clearly, we are moving beyond fear because fear is just a smell, a pheromone—a basic response that nature hands out as default factory settings. Its purpose like an invisible invitation, signaling to night predators that your flesh and blood fits well between their teeth and will digest nicely in their bellies. No. No. No. I begin to feel our old fear glands simultaneously turn vestigial and wither as we are literally taking this trip to the next level.

Totty and English Black Dahlia have their arms out the windows, throwing glow sticks at the dirt biker's heads and faces until they eventually screw off and speed away down a side street. We are changing, transforming. And because of our continuous feasting on magic potions and moonshine, we are SUDDENLY and UNIFORMLY evolving by the minute. Your minute, not ours, because time is not here anymore. Not for us. In this form, what we can do with two seconds—one Mississippi, two Mississippi—would be described by lesser humans as something in the realm of SUPERNATURE. Nocturnal creatures of the highest order, roaming within a secret world of secret colours, aiming toward the spot on our pyrate map that says THERE BE DRAGONS because we are lawless by nature, and dragons no longer scare us because having the ability to see higher truths creates higher forms of life. And it happens in two seconds.

Between 00:45 and 01:30

The girls, to no surprise, want to go to the Hippodrome, 1700 Main Street, a historical landmark. The former Paramount Theatre that, as of this summer, has been refurbished, rebranded, and reopened as THE nightclub of the city and immediately established as a top-spot major haunt, a late-night jaunt for dudes not to daunt or taunt, but to vaunt while being nonchalant with dames who WANT TO FLAUNT.

Savage says, "We're here."

Hippodrome is spelled out vertically down the building's facade in white letters on red squares in big bold font.

Savage mounts the short bus on the sidewalk. "Wait, did I just drive us? Why don't I remember that?" His words communicate true panic.

"'LAVISH,'" English Black Dahlia curates. "That's how a local paper described it. And it is. For the sole reason that the millennium is nigh, and *the future* is an idea but more like a prize to win, and the prize is the winner getting to define it, which means you're also claiming it. So in a sense, you could say that there's an unspoken struggle happening where we all want to give birth to the fucking twenty-first century."

"Makes sense," Totty says, studying her hand.

And regarding hands, I realize I am holding Rebecca's, or she is holding mine. *We are both holding, fifty-fifty.* And she tells me this with a glance.

We all shiver. A clear signal similar to a whistle or a bell or a gunshot that tells all parties the games have officially commenced, and we are now witnessing all the COLOURS, all types: the old hues that have been long ago established and our newly invented ones that taste identical to alien fever dreams mixed with gourmet cotton candy, our minds evoking God's own prism, humming eternally like a tuning fork somehow enchanted with a soul and a universal sentience.

"And prize means gift means PRESENT. So the *present* is the future," English Black Dahlia says, putting a finer point to her previous observation. She says this smiling, her voice a blend of giddy, raw, and relieved as if she just bellowed out a MONSTER orgasm.

Then without missing a beat, she grabs Totty, and the two start aggressively making out. Sexy! Both broads are suddenly hungry for the taste of girl. Beyond words now, but their bodies are conversing. Ebb and flow. Their bodies cannot get close enough together, but it's almost as if their hips have a magnetic field for the other. They are squeezing tits, breathing heavily as angsty tongues wrestle vainly for contact with the other's uvula. And when this is apparent, they counter head-tilt and resume devouring each other's mouths.

Savage says, "Where'd did Erik go?"

But I'm not listening. Nope. I'm watching this lesbian shit just happening right now before me in our pyrate-sped bus. Their shirts are getting lifted, first a little then a little more and then WHOA! Those horny hands of theirs are under cotton, grabbing handfuls of thick boob-meat. When the nipples are tugged, Totty lifts her tongue out to open and exposes her neck to allow English Black Dahlia full access to that soft neck, which feels so damn good when sucked and nibbled on, and instantly, Totty squeals and whimpers. Obviously, it feels so good, her body wants her to cry, laugh, and moan. So much pleasure for her right now, she's vibrating. Tongue to the business side of a nine-volt and you know she's a girl that squirts.

Savage says, "CLASS! Hello! Classic Fucking Nick! Have you seen our bass player?"

I say "oh my god" or "Jesus Christ" or "holy shit." I don't know what sentences or phrases are coming out. It's more like I'm passing words, but whatever I say, I actually mean "PLEASE DON'T STOP!"

How Classic Nick actually reacts is by flashing Savage dual hand-horns while screaming "FUCKING HUNGRY LIKE THE WOLF!" before letting his tongue out to hang like Gene Simmons or a drooling canine and then starts cheering the two girls with loud whoops and hollers that, to the surprise of those present, dissipate in volume almost immediately and doesn't bounce within the Blunderbus interior with a deafening echo. It is as if the vehicle was designed specifically to withstand the barrage of loud obnoxious sounds by the mentally absent.

"There it is! It's happening!" I think I'm screaming, but it doesn't fucking matter because now the hands are going under the denim! "FUCK YES! FUCK YES! FUCK YES! FUCK YES!"

Wet sounds. Labia minor and major parting like the hand mixing of meat loaf before hitting the oven, and it's so goddamn gushy, the bus almost feels humid. And then more wet sounds follow from another salty wave of natural pussy wetness. Then the sounds turn hard like sloppy churning from submerged fingers, bending knuckles for simulated girth. The noises become deeper. Gawd damn! Maybe more than two fingers, and soon enough, there's speed and deliberate tempos (slow-medium-fast), and it's real fast. Dirty-girl fast. Come on and cum fast! Rinse-cycle fast. Running in flip-flops fast. Mexican laborer fast. I want the smell to fill the room fast, so fucking cum now, and do it fast! Noises indicating a soon release of pressure that immediately proceeds spastic gyrations and accompanying verbal sounds that tell the owner of the wet fingers they are aware their hand is tired from straining to juice this RIPE fruit, but rest assured, the sweet nectar is COMING! And there's so much juice, so nutritious, so rest your tired hand. Wait.

"I'm jizzing!" Classic Nick moans out like a drowning victim that has just been resuscitated from CPR, and the lungs push out the trapped water so he can breathe. And he breathes hard and rhythmically, for he is alive, and taking in lungfuls of air never felt so right. And like the shiver from before, they shiver again as a unit. But instead of a shiver, it's more like a tremor that purges all the tension out of my whole being so much so when I take a sip of Pedialyte, I take two because my soul is also thirsty from busting so fucking hard that cumming transcended the physical realm, managing to secure a fist-clench of spiritual for good fucking measure. Gawd damn. I think that also cured some mental affliction I didn't know I had, like a childhood trauma was just made right, and the crying child I once was has just be given a cookie and their boo-boos kissed.

My inner self has adjusted one notch, and now the little bubble that illustrates how level I am in my life just floated a little closer to the middle spot of the gauge.

And yup, there's a fucking sizeable load right there on the back of the bench before me. It's a lot of cum, like the amount in the little metal cup that comes with a lobster; but instead of delicious hot melted dairy butter, it is a bird-shit splatter of my baby batter and hot dribbly pastry icing. A true jizz-oyster really, because the consistency is super fucking thick, and I know if I had fired that nut into a gash, I'd definitely be welcoming the twenty-first century as a soon-to-be dad.

Fuck that. I can practically hear them swimming. Actually, I think I really hear them moving. My tadpoles wanting so bad to germinate a female egg, but instead, they are semen on a sinking ship, going down on retard benching. And it looks the way you would imagine a hocked wad of diseased-coloured phlegm making its way down a pane of glass would look, leaving a snail trail along the way. Did the trip turn on me? On us?

Us? Where is everybody?

Then the colours disappeared.

"Rebecca!" I scream, standing in the middle of the street. "Rebecca, where are you? Tell me where you are!"

I immediately notice two still silhouettes standing under the stout-stone underpass by the new nightclub. Is that Erik and Savage? The drugs surely have affected my legs as I seem to have a hard time walking. The colours are gone now. Long gone. And the magic they brought that makes everything so light and playful and full of life is gone too, and now I'm in a vulnerable state. My legs drop from under me, and I hit the ground. I can hear whispering within the shadows, or maybe it's coming *from* the shadows themselves. *Themselves?* What the fuck am I saying? I try to stand, but it is useless. I can only crawl.

Lost time. Lapses within the fabric. Look at your surroundings. Nothing makes sense.

"Guys?" I weakly cry to the silhouettes. "Is that you, guys? Please answer me if that's you! The drugs have turned on us. All binge-tripping this year has done something to our minds, and now we exist as something *unnatural*!"

The word DAMNATION enters my thoughts. *Is this real?*

I'm crawling down Main Street over all road pebbles and real fine particles of what feels like glass dust that embed right into my palms. I am inching toward the underpass to join my shadowed friends, and there is a part of me that thinks I've been doing this for a very long time.

It is not *hell*. It is just the drugs.

Maybe their shadows have gone rogue and left their bodies to exist independently in the third dimension. Or perhaps the shadows have just taken over, and now their souls belong to the night, and soon yours will too. Play spooky games, win spooky prizes.

I am crawling fast now. Almost too fast. Impossibly fast. I don't understand what is going on. My eyes are shaking. I feel a contorting happening from within and HEAT. So much heat is now radiating through my body. Dark rivers of magma. My bones glow white, sizzling embers. My jaw, voltage. My teeth grow an intelligence that immediately communicates to my brain that they are angry at the moonlight. I cannot scream—wait, at the *moonlight*? Fuck! I feel my spine extend and droop down like it's taking a *living* shit made of cartilage. My mouth—whatever fuck my mouth. It's my tongue. My tongue cannot make words, and when I try to scream at the silhouettes again, they have changed!

I don't believe what I am seeing! Hearing Erik's words gives me a moment of relief. Savage's too, but it's strange somehow. Stranger is the noise in my fucking head that's not part of me. It's being injected into me or projected or transmitted. Yes! An awful noise, like a frequency instilling anguish, and I know its true purpose is to drive me insane. And I know it's coming from the moon because this is what happens when God's law has been broken, and I know now that I broke it with excessive moonlight and consuming the menstrual blood!

I lift my new head and release a deep and vicious howl that shuts the moon up.

I think I bit Erik the last time we had practice. Was that yesterday? I am uncertain how time works now, and that's why he's been sickly and reading that old book on werewolves. He knew I spread my curse to him, and he was trying to prevent the *transformation*.

My new wolf eyes have crescent moons reflected in the pupils that glow like hellfire. And just like your body's blood never knowing its true colour until it gets released from your inner dark, the real colour of night is a very ancient hue of red. That is the true colour of reality. And even though humans don't see it, they sense it's there. It is why people fear the night.

Savage too is a werewolf now. "Since you and Erik were both cursed and the fact that a band is like a tribe or a CULT, I was given the choice to join you bastards. So I figured why not, right? At the end of the day, aren't musicians PACK ANIMALS? Besides, it'll make for a helluva chapter in our future tell-all, am I right?"

"*Who* presented you with the choice?" Erik asks.

Savage just shrugs like "who fucking cares, dude?"

"Regardless, I'm glad the three of us are in it together."

We chest-bump and stand upright on our hind legs within the dark of the underpass. And, suddenly, the Moon begins *transmitting* that horrible frequency again that sears into our heads, causing pain so bad, we yelp and growl and fall off our back legs onto the pavement and start rolling around.

I yell to the boys, "We have to howl to make it stop!"

So together, as a pack, we run out into the open street until the moon is visible. We stop, arch our backs, aim our broad snouts at the moon (which looks so much different when you're a werewolf), and with everything we can muster, we release the most ferociously primal HOWLS that downtown Springfield has ever heard. **"Ooow-wooo!"**

For us werewolves, howling at the moon is a war cry. A nocturnal philosophy. A direct communication that we hear the demands of our curse, but we have the self-respect to carry out our obligations with class, passion, and showmanship.

The howling, of course, makes the noise stop, and the pain in our heads halt while a new pain begins to manifest in our stomachs that simultaneously makes our bellies groan aggressively, indicating the moral debit of our curse: **the hunger pangs**.

"We must feed!" I say. "***The BOSS*** requires it."

Next Chapter

"Let's do 'Bark at the Moon' as we hunt but not invoking any Ozzy. Let's really make it our own! Ready? One, two—one, two, three, four!"

We ditch the Blunderbus along with the girls to stalk the Springfield streets, prowling the proximal, resolving to scout our nearby streetscapes, looking for the right choice to find our first night's meal, yes, but also taking into consideration the cost of our choice in regard to when the sunlight returns and the sheep wake up and come to realize the true toll of the night, who got fed to the wolves and who did not.

The boys started running down Lynden Street, past the long stone Union Station, past Gino's Pizza to Mardi Gras, a popular Springfield bar and venue of adult entertainment, known amongst all the local strip clubs as being considered, by far, the most reputable and higher end choice the city has to offer. The boys, in a disturbingly agitated and frenzied state, stormed the entrance, successfully bypassing the front-end attendant, the manager, and two of the security guards. They managed to confiscate and consume multiple drinks and then rush two of the dancers on stage who were assaulted for almost one whole minute. The dancers, during this minute, were subjected to being groped and manhandled and forcibly kissed by the boys until several patrons, along with the whole security team, were able to subdue the boys long enough to throw them outside.

"Fuck your mother's record collection!"

"You faggots are more overpaid than a New York Yankee!"

Outside, Classic Nick and Erik spat at the men while Savage began micturating and tossing palmfuls of urine at security. It's important to note here that all three boys were in a state of complete undress. They soon ran off and were able to evade the subsequent street sweeps done by almost all the responding officers, which included cruisers, motorcycles, and one rookie on a bicycle.

Of course, the piggies didn't catch us! They couldn't find us! Lycanthropes, especially those of us native to the New England regions and some of the northern territories of Canada, are known to employ crude cloaking abilities for short periods of time.

We sing Metallica's "Of Wolf and Man," and naturally, we know all the lyrics.

You must be able to see the Boss's true face (like his actual face) to be able to reject all nearby light to turn on your outer dark shell. And that's only something a handful of all active werewolves in these certain regions can do. We werewolves have all sorts of powers.

They took off most of their clothes earlier that evening. So when they did decide to drive down to the Hippodrome Nightclub, they were, for the most part, in their undergarments. So when that point of the night inevitably arrived, when the totality of all the drugs ingested finally took full effect, it was only Erik who was fully clothed, and that was, of course, quickly changed.

We each play our respective air instruments, and I swear to fucking God, we actually hear the fucking music.

Erik says, "Nietzsche said, 'Those who were seen dancing were thought to be insane by those who couldn't hear the music.'"

When it becomes obvious that we have successfully thwarted the piggies—I knew we would. No, WE knew we would. But when the coast is clear, we run to a nearby dumpster behind a restaurant. We dive in and tear apart plastic bags and devour all foodstuffs, throwing out anything else that's not edible.

Savage finds a dead cat. This makes us belly laugh. Then we find another. We toss them around, doing funny things with them like making them dance or pretending to fuck them or giving them funny voices and having them fuck themselves. We sing the chorus to "Scary Monsters (And Super Creeps)," channeling less David Bowie but Kurt Cobain instead. Then we howl and take off to find more to eat.

They decide to keep the cat carcasses and continue their psychotic trip, running nude through the streets. They soon come across a homeless man pushing a shopping cart filled with cans, which they knock over. And they begin denting and caving in the cart by jumping on it.

We tell the filthy fuck that we are werewolves, and he nodded and said he could tell. We tell him we can transfer unto him the power of the wolf, but he has to do something for us, that he has to fuck one of the dead cats. He sobs a little then agrees and drops down his pants, but he starts sobbing more when he says he's too old and that his dick can't get hard. We tell him to use his imagination and picture plump ladies like Ricki Lake or Monica Lewinsky, but still sobbing, he says he doesn't know who they are. Instead, he'll suck all three of our dicks for some werewolf powers.

Erik gets angry. "That wasn't the deal, you human turd!" And he starts hitting him with one of the dead cats, but his pants are still around his ankles, so keeps stumbling until he falls over. Erik then shoves the cat's rotting asshole in his face. "EAT IT, YOU FUCKING HUMAN TURD!"

Savage takes a chewy bite out of the cat's throat, leans over, and vomits in the face of the human turd.

I lean down and whisper in his ear, "Fuck Sammy Hagar." But instead of whispering, I scream it because I want to appropriately articulate this sentiment. And again, we take off, screaming in unison the lyrics to "Running with the Devil."

Savage screams, "Holy shit! I think I can actually hear the song playing!" He screams this, pointing his massive claw to the moon. "Fucking DJ Moonstruck!" And a snap of the fingers later, we hear it too! We understand the advanced science of musical delivery by way of moonbeams almost immediately. "It all makes sense!"

We take a moment to groove on a street corner, taking turns pole dancing on the streetlamp, leaping in the air, trying to touch the moon—which, of course, will never happen. But it's fun to pretend that celestial bodies are in the reach of our *manos de hombre lobo*. We want to reach up and pluck a star out of the sky, roll it around between our paws, then flick it away like a freshly picked booger.

"I would pull black holes out of the sky all day and eat them raw like wild berries."

Erik somehow has a chain of glow sticks, and Savage and I die laughing from the image of a loup-garou TWIRLING. "You are the picture of madness, Erik!" Pantomiming a snapshot. Then Savage does a fucking back flip, so I now have to do something, so I leap up with wide legs and land in the foreground, doing the perfect splits as Erik shimmies betwixt us, giving that glow lasso a rodeo spin.

We bite the glow sticks with our fangs and, like champagne, we douse our fur with light.

The Boss changes tracks, and now "Wild One" by Iggy Pop is playing loud with the most perfect sound imaginable. Eagerly received, goddamn birthday cake for the ears. "FUCK YEAH!" is screamed from somewhere deep. And we yelp and jump and high-five, playfully hitting each other before we shout, "Goddamn, I love being a werewolf!"

The boys run into a nearby parking garage where they immediately set their sights on the same purple Volkswagen Beetle. They charge their target full speed, run over to the passenger side, crouch down, and without a word spoken, they heave the car upward and drop it with a grinding crunch onto its driver side. They let out goofy guffaws then begin pushing against the undercarriage and start rocking the car back and forth, back and forth, and there's glass cracking and more crunching and the unseen rattling of loosening parts. The energy builds until the time is right when they let go and the car lurches forward in quick motion, pauses for a moment, then with the final jolt of remaining momentum, lands with a creaking slow collapse onto its roof. Glass shatters and those unseen loose parts instantly wobble free and drop like pinballs rolling down predestined mechanical pathways. Under the new inverse of weight, the roof continues to condense into itself like a beer can being gradually crushed. The car's volume doesn't seem to stop settling until a rumble emits from somewhere within the bug and all movement ceases, save for the diminishing spin of the tires. This gives the appearance of the twitching from an upended insect whose instinct to crawl is the last thing to die.

The boys, laughing wholeheartedly, take in the sight of their victory. There's a Kafka joke to be made, and naturally, Erik makes it, but it falls flat because the situation is beyond any witty observation. It's beyond words. Beyond language. The image of the dead beetle is the perfect final offering to the night. To the full sturgeon moon of August 1999.

We declare the Boss has been satiated, and soon enough, the black evening curtain on the eastern horizon begins to lift. We watch the Boss's face—still stoic, of course, but now with a hint of quiet satisfaction, knowing he can rest easy. That trust to carry out the mission was placed in the appropriate hands.

The Boss's face freezes with the first sunbeam. This happens as our systems start ebbing away from the animal form: bone, teeth, snout, claws. Like a window being shut. Then our fur and eyes vanish in fuck-all of a second as the Boss winks at us then disappears as the retarded sun and all the lame shit it represents rises in the sky, giving security to whole world of faggy-ass sheep so they can keep eating grass, indistinguishable within the herd. Stupid lives that contain no magic, no lust, no passion, and no angry sharp teeth.

PART 2

NEXT CHAPTER

September 2

We play a venue in Worcester called House of Cards. We only the play the new songs from our upcoming album. A nerd from the *Boston Globe* is there and invites us to his table. He tells us he's been aware of us for some time now and that our new set is what he describes as "surreal slaughterhouse punk" (whatever the fuck that means).

He says, "I'm working on a piece about Y2K and end-of-the-world dread and how it is affecting the arts, and I would love to add some Fuck'd for Life flavor into the story."

During the interview, Erik tells the reporter that our pyrate theme is no gimmick, that we take our pyracy deadly serious.

The reporter is intrigued. "Care to elaborate?" he says, gesturing with his pen.

Erik fires up a cigarette. "We embrace lawlessness every day! It's a Springfield thing. We got crime up the wazoo there. Roving dirt bike gangs that are super aggressive. I drove into a pack of them once with a car I stole, and those bastards still kept getting up. They took a long time to die."

The reporter laughs nervously. "Surely you're joking."

Erik laughs. "Yeah. I'm fucking with you. None of them died. At least, I don't think. Oh, but we do drive around and steal packages that FedEx or UPS delivers."

The reporter looks uncomfortable. "So you guys are *porch pyrates?*"

"You know, from online shopping—eBay and Amazon. That's why I've been reading so much. It's a lot of books, which is good. I'm glad people are still reading."

The boys disavow everything played on the radio, even the songs they like that get airtime are temporarily tainted by its broadcasting. It is their assertion that radio commercials are most likely the leading cause of miscarriage in North America.

We start spray-painting "Fuck Staind" all over Springfield. We start rumors they are Holocaust deniers.

September 4

We play a house show in Dorchester. Someone Erik knows but not really. A friend of a friend of his ex-wife. He's an asshole when it comes to giving detail. For example, that's when I first learned Erik had an ex-wife.

I asked, "When the hell were you married?"

"Oh, it was just for a couple months. Right around the time I was a cabbie in NYC."

"When the fuck were you a cabbie in NYC?"

He scoffs incredulously. "Around the time I was married. I just said this. Pay attention, dude. I hate repeating myself." He walks away, and frustrated, I punch a hole in the wall just as Savage was turning a corner. He looks at the hole.

The owner of the spacious Dorchester house, a red-nosed silverback of a man with an orange mustache called Sly, told us to go ham and be as loud as possible. He was hosting a small get-together, maybe a birthday or a family reunion or just a casual Saturday fiesta. Only a few of the ladies attending were doable, but even then, their fucking accents—their laughs! Christ almighty. One of them had a fucking neck thicker than Savage's! Cable veins like extension cords that pulsed and jutted out as she consumed an entire party-size bag of Doritos.

There was another woman who, judging from the uniform she was wearing, was either a homeless mailman or had just survived a house-fire moment before arriving to the party. She was drinking cold soup from a can and smoking a cigar.

The first song we play is an older song, "There's No Asian Pyrates" (because they can't say ARRR!). And it's an instant hit with the crowd, and they start cheering and hollering. After the song, I tell them that we appreciate Bostonians and their casual racism, and someone shouts, "Play 'Freebird'!" And I say, "My point exactly!"

We play a few more songs, including a new one I wrote: "I Eat Pussy Period." It's a raw, in-your-face fuck anthem with some noise and distortion elements, a lot of screaming, and a driving beat of double bass drum. Near the end, I put an Alka-Seltzer tablet and a few blood capsules in my mouth to gurgle out a frothy geyser of gore right when the song crescendos. As performers, it's important for us to take risks and test the crowd and find their limits. Some bands would probably avoid pushing it too far, especially at a private show like this, but that is not our policy. And in fact, we notice some dudes in the back walking out, but fuck it. I'm not saying what we are doing is art, but we sure like it.

During a break, Savage takes me aside. "There's something off going on in this house. I feel it in my lower tailbone."

"Hmm," I say, rubbing the hair on my chin. "You know, it's funny you mention that. Did you happen to notice that all the men have been sneaking out one by one?"

Savage smiles. "What are you thinking, gay sex? Irish Catholic husbands doing it on the DL?"

I give him a blank stare. "Why is that where your mind always goes? Secret gay orgies."

"Oh, fuck off! You were thinking the same thing!" Savage says in a tone.

And because it was spoken, those three magic words and POOF! Erik appears like a fucking apparition. "You guys talking about gay sex orgies again?"

I jump. "Jesus Christ!"

"Class thinks there's a mustached blow-fest happening covertly somewhere in this house," Savage says with a tantalizing eyebrow raise.

"Yup," I say sarcastically. "That's exactly what I said. Verbatim."

Erik waves it off. "I wouldn't worry about any of that. They are more afraid of you than you are of them."

I'm shaking my head violently. "The fuck are you talking about? Are you confusing raccoons with homosexuals?"

Erik scoffs, "Hey! I'm not afraid of raccoons, okay? I just don't trust them! They look like bandits, and they wash their food before eating it. Fuck is that about?"

I turn and punch another hole in a nearby wall.

As we were about to start jamming again after Savage briefly retunes his drum set, Sly appears again, his face maintaining a frustrated expression that seems—to some degree or another—permanent, like he's always a little constipated.

He approaches us, heavily perspiring. "You boys have to leave right now!"

"Sly," Erik says like they're brothers. "What are you talking about? What's wrong? Not digging our sound?"

Sly draws in a deep breath. "The dogs! Whatever it is about you, I don't know, but they clearly know you're here, and they're in the basement and won't stop barking. We can't get them to stop long enough to fight! It's almost if they are afraid of youse, and that fear is uniting them! Which defeats the purpose! We can't have that!"

"Are you fucking kidding me?"

"Dog fighting!" Savage screams. "I knew I sensed something!"

"Wait!" Erik says, getting closer to Sly. "What about the bet?"

"What bet, Erik? What fucking bet? You knew about this?" My hands are trembling.

Sly looks at me. "He said you knew! He said you guys wanted to bet your proceeds tonight on Brad the Pit Bull! He was very adamant about that. He said youse knew!"

Savage is looking around, meticulously scanning the Dorchester homestead. For what, exactly, I don't know.

"Erik, I'm going to kill you!" My voice is quivering.

He looks at me. "Oh, take it easy! It was a lock! Which is why Sweaty Sly Guy here is trying to gyp us because he knows we were going to win! Dirty pool, Sly. Shame on you. I thought I knew you better than that!"

I shout to myself, "And I thought it was a gay orgy you were hiding!"

Savage points at me. "Aha! I knew it! See, your mind goes there too. Birds of a feather suck cock together." He looks confused. "Wait. I don't think that's the expression."

Sly looks confused amidst the banter but focuses back on Erik. "Oh, fuck you, Erik! We were cellmates for barely a month before I was transferred! We hardly fucking know each other! But I know enough to know I don't like youse, and the dogs definitely don't like youse! Your fucking presence has them spooked! Now c'mon. Pack up your shit and get out!"

I look at Erik. "Fucking cellmates? What the fuck, Erik!"

Erik shrugs and Sly tosses a stack of rubber banded bills at him. "Now go! And you're lucky I'm paying youse. I know one of you guys clogged my toilet!"

Savage raises his hand. "Sorry about that. My diet has been insane lately."

Sly starts the momentum of walking away.

"Sly, wait!"

He stops and looks at me.

"So it's just dog fighting? No DL gay sex shit? Entertaining the wives while the husbands"—I make a simple hand gesture that's somehow meant to represent repressed homosexual butt-fucking—"you know?"

Sly looks around coolly at what remains of the crowd, who are trying not to pay attention but totally transfixed. He adjusts his shirt collars. "Mind your business."

The boys reject Powerman 5000, Kid Rock, Godsmack, Limp Bizkit, as well as the music genres of post-grunge and nu-metal. At their shows, they emphatically denounce marriage, mortgages, monotheism, sobriety, modern civilization, firefighters, doing your taxes, the age of consent, and people with 401Ks.

We start an online petition demanding all depictions of Jesus Christ be changed to him with slicked-back hair, a Fu Manchu, and a soul patch. We tell people that Jesus's body wasn't placed into a tomb—that after the crucifixion, it was fed to wild dogs. We read it in a book.

September 6 or 7

Actually, we are not sure. Let's just say date indeterminate. So!

Have you ever heard of the Bridgewater Triangle? It's a pie slice of an area purported with all sorts of paranormal shit. It is roughly a 200-square-mile spread in southeastern Massachusetts that includes the cities of Bridgewater, Taunton, Freetown, and at the center of this X-Files bullshit, a vast wetland called Hockomock Swamp, which Erik tells me means "place where spirits dwell" in Algonquin. He said he read in a book that original English settlers called this place Devil's Swamp, and the cunt waited till Savage peed in the bog to tell him that much of the area was used as a sacred burial site.

"Congratulations, dude. You fucking desecrater! You are probably cursed now!" Erik said, chuckling and eating a Drake's coffee cake, then tossing the wrapper in the marsh.

That was days ago. I think.

Whatever metric of whatever amount of time exactly, we are not entirely sure. Fuck it. But in this unknown period of time, we've been camping in the Blunderbus that's parked in the Freetown State Forest, also located in the Bridgewater Triangle.

We wanted to include some impromptu spooky tourism during a chunk of off time while on this half-baked New England road tour we set up literally last fucking minute, all to promote this new album. I think our next set is in Providence, Rhode Island, on the tenth. Wait!

"Guys, I think this is eighth!" I announce after doing some mental math. "You know, I really think we fucked up. We should have saved those flares."

Savage screams, "The eighth! We better sober up! Totty is going to think I am dead."

Erik rests his hand on his shoulder. "You will be dead after the bones of the dead Indian warriors reassemble to cut off your fucking head with a tomahawk and then torment your lost spirit for all eternity."

"Nooo!" Savage screams, running off bare-assed into a thick pocket of wooding. "Shut up, Erik!" Then from a distance a few moments later, he shouts, "You're giving me diarrhea again!"

"Will you stop fucking with him! You are literally driving him insane!"

It's true. Savage has been breaking down mentally. After Erik told him of his old-world malediction, it took me ten minutes of consoling to get him out of a tree that he climbed so we wouldn't see him cry, even though he was clearly audible. When he came down, he had black eyeliner streaks running from his eyes down his face, which, whatever that's about, is none of my business. But it's a new development. That's for sure.

"Hey, fuck you!" Erik shouts, his pee-pee wiggling as he gesticulates. "That piece of shit disrespected my native ancestry! I have the right to curse whoever the fuck I want!"

"Oh, you're Native American now?" I snort. "I thought you were Armenian Italian?"

He shrugs. "Armenian Italian Indian. What? We have a community. It's a popular enough mix." He says this then takes a chug from the tequila bottle with the shoelace tied around the neck.

"Maybe take a break with that!"

He grimaces one side of his face like he's disgusted. "Oh, I get it. Now that you know I am Indian, now I am an alcoholic! Is that what you are fucking telling me, you fucking insensitive prick!"

I sigh. "You're not part Indian—are you, Erik?"

He scoffs then squints. "Maybe Dutch? I don't know. My father said my grandmother was raped a lot. Kind of a hot-topic issue actually. Appreciate you not making light of it. You don't hear me talking about the Japanese internment camps and the atrocities your grandparents suffered during that dark period, huh? Do you, *Classic fucking Nick?*"

My mouth is probably agape. I just stare at him. "You do know I am not Japanese, right?"

He's bewildered. "What!"

"Yup. Not of any Asian descent at all, actually."

By his expression, he's clearly shocked. "No shit! Wow, think you know someone." And he starts doing an aimless nude stroll, still drinking from the shoelaced bottle. He starts hum-singing "Cruel Summer" by Bananarama when a branch snaps and Savage comes falling out of a nearby tree.

It was—whatever—how many nights ago we made the plan to sneak into the Taunton State Hospital, a psychiatric hospital that opened in 1854 and was later decommissioned in the 1970s, which has since fallen into a state of negligent disrepair. Formerly called the State Lunatic Hospital at Taunton, it treated two serial killers during its run. Anthony Santo and Jane Toppan, both of which died at the facility, which is another factoid Erik waited to disclose at the last minute. But most certainly, it wouldn't have deterred us one bit. The Taunton State Hospital is also located within the notorious Bridgewater Triangle and is claimed to be haunted by the ghosts of former patients. There's also been a few dozen reports of satanic cults using the place for sacrifices and blood rituals and shit, which, as it turns out, is a common thread reported from most of the locales within this paranormal slice of Massachusetts pie.

An abandoned loony bin set in an infamously sinister landscape—how hell could we pass this up? After spending hours drinking tequila and setting off fireworks at the Devil's Swamp, we decided to set sail, under the guise of night, to the abandoned house of lunacy.

Our plan was to sneak into the abandoned building with our camcorder and some instruments and get some footage for a music video. Fucking genius. Driving there in the Blunderbus, we listened to the albums *Moontower* by Swedish progressive death metal musician San Swano and Slayer's *Diabolus in Musica* while Erik, and I took turns giving each other a couple of quick tattoos.

"We are running out of places to tag ya, Erik. You are starting to look like a schizophrenic's journal that's been left in the rain."

"You're pretty much the same, Class! At least, mine look a little better. Yours are mostly real shitty looking."

"Those are from you!" I shout as Savage hits a pothole and the needle goes rogue, and Erik looks at me like he just shits on the floor. He resumes, a moment later, tattooing my leg.

"Kinda funny that you, the best artist out of the three of us, has the shittiest tattoos."

"Well, your hands are about as steady—" I pause because I don't want to name the actor that played the character Scott Howard. But I can't think of anything clever, and the clock is ticking. "As steady as an unbalanced washing machine."

Erik snorts. "Wow. Good one," he says sarcastically.

I add, "Not to mention, Savage is scared of holding anything that vibrates." And this makes Erik laugh.

Savage, at the wheel, is suddenly animated. He turns back to look at us. "I'm not scared. I already explained that it just reminds me of when I was a kid, and my mother would hold me down and make me smell her sex toys." He pauses and sniffles after saying this. "Which is also the same reason I don't like Dijon mustard."

Erik and I share a look. He rolls his eyes, and I gesture a finger twirl at my temple that's meant to represent crazy. To this, Erik replies, "Yeah, no kidding."

I tattoo three little pictures on Erik's back: a bridge, a small wavy body of water, and a triangle. And on my leg, Erik tattooed, "Savage's mum is a cum dumpster."

"Real nice," I say sardonically. And when Savage sees it—or rather when Erik tells him and then he demands to see it—there's a sudden clenching of his fists, and I think he's finally going to break down and beat the shit out of Erik and I'm going to have to use the tranquilizer gun that we stole that time from the ranger's outpost near the Quabbin and fire a dart in Savage's ass in an attempt to stop that gorilla from turning Erik into a puddle. But as it happens, he doesn't. Savage remains still. He just swallows hard and pushes the injustice deep down into his core and unclenches his fist.

He stops the bus. "We are here," he says. "Hodges Avenue in Taunton, Massachusetts."

Erik and I eagerly look through the windows at the hospital pitched in genre-film darkness. First, high up, we see the cupola. That's what Erik calls the dome that towers over the building's facade. We drive around to the back for more cover.

We decide only to bring the camera and not to bring any instruments lest the piggies interrupt and we need to make a quick dash out of there. The camera was a Sony Handycam with NightShot that we got last year after we saw a news report on the camera having the ability to see through clothes and bikinis. It took some tampering with, but eventually, Savage was able to do something to the filter or something and then hell yeah! We got that thing rockin' and rollin', and we initially used it to film all the fat-assed Spanish babes at Five Mile Pond in Springfield. But the scene there changed when cops found that decapitated corpse, and we moved to Puffer's Pond in Amherst and filmed a bunch of X-rated shit with all those dripping-wet college broads in their two-pieces. We also brought it to Woodstock '99, but most of the chicks there were, for the most part, running around naked anyway.

Never underestimate the power of music.

The last time we used the camera for X-Ray-ted purposes was at that nursing home with a bunch of old pieces of shit in their very thin nightgowns or hospital gowns. Holy shit! That was fucking GNARLY! That was scarier than the fucking *Blair Witch Project*! It became clear to us that humans, when they get old, start to rot like fruit. It was the same nursing home where that asshole couch-surfer Rand's grandmother was left to die—another useless fact about his family he wouldn't shut up about.

We were eventually able to find his dumb two-hundred-year-old nana and tell her that we wanted to film her to surprise him for his birthday, and she's probably demented and just as retarded as him, and so she went along with it and Jesus fucking Christ! We had her stand by the window and filmed her singing "Happy Birthday" in her nightie. And later, we secretly dosed Rand with a fuckload of LSD, tied him to a chair, and forced him to watch the video of her shitty naked body. He screamed and cried for it to stop, but he must have liked it because he became visibly aroused. Afterward, we showed him some bonus footage of Erik resting his balls on her sleeping face after her meds kicked in. Rand definitely didn't like that part, and his erection subsided, and he started weeping. Funny part is Erik got a rash on his sack from that! Just ten seconds of testicular contact with her face! Fucking weird family. And of course, Rand moved out the next day.

It took us about twenty-five minutes of stumbling around the abandoned hospital to find a door that actually led to something. It seems a good portion of the structure was collapsing in on itself, and a few doors were boarded up. And when Savage kicked through other doors, beyond the doorways, into the hallways, they were filled with so much debris, and it was so dark, it would make traversing the space a fuck-show. And, no doubt, one of us would fall and break our ass.

In the end, we didn't end up filming anything because as we made our way to the front of the building to the double doors at the hospital's facade and right when Savage heaved his gorilla frame into the doors, it became clear we weren't getting in, but not because of any debris or compromised roofing this time. It was because of the reverberation that Savage's forced entry sent through the rest of the building, which, at first, was almost inaudible. We barely heard it. But it quickly became apparent the vibrations were gradually increasing, and soon enough, the tremoring turned into sounds of slow destruction that resonated the loudest above our heads.

"Run!"

We hauled ass back in the direction of the Blunderbus, just in time to turn around and see the dome disappear into the bulk of the structure, leaving behind a cloud of dust illuminated only by the moon in its waning crescent phase.

Smash cut! And I am ripping the tequila bottle out of Erik's hand. I scream, "WHY ARE WE STILL CAMPING HERE! I'M SICK OF THE WOODS! I AM SICK OF THE TRIANGLE! WE ARE LEAVING NOW!"

I am suddenly overcome with a real need for pavement and electric light and that the novelty of the spooky camping trip (don't forget drunken) in the Freetown State Forest—our third and final destination in this Bridgewater Triangle trilogy—needs to be done now, now, now.

I continue screaming. "Fuck you, you stupid haunted forest! Fuck you, trees! You're the stupidest fucking trees in the state! Fuck you, solitude rock or suicide rock! You're a stupid rock, and that's why people die near you. Because you suck!"

I am kicking plants and spitting on trees and sobbing hysterically when I scream all this. I hate camping. I loathe the outdoors. I want to meet Mother Nature in a chatroom and sweet-talk her to meeting me in real life. "Oh sure. I'm a chipper dude! I love bugs! And sloths! And those giant bats with the heads of foxes! I'm a big fan of your massive oeuvre, you stupid bitch. Oh! Did I say *stupid bitch*? Well, I surely didn't mean that. You know I love you. It was a typo! Now come over right now! I live in the Red House on Mulberry Street, Springfield, Massachusetts!"

And when she comes over, I fucking slam the door behind her because I had been hiding for the past two hours, waiting for her to walk through my door. I lock the deadbolt. And she knows, just by looking at me, that this guy is sick of her fucking shit, and I tell her as much.

"I am so sick of your shit, you stupid bitch, so I am going to rape the fucking shit out of you!" I grab her by her hair and slam her head into the fridge. Then I open the freezer, and putting her stupid fucking head in the jam, I slam the freezer door on her stupid cunt head that I pull out. I bring her face close to mine, and she probably spits some blood at my face, but the fucking retarded cunt is too stupid to realize I love the taste of female blood. I fucking love it!

That's when I'll kiss Mother Nature hard and press my face hard into hers and invite her tongue into my mouth, where I bite the tip off so I can suck a heavier stream of her blood. Then I'll grab a dirty paring knife out of the sink and stick it in her eye socket, being sure to wiggle it around enough until the eye is completely destroyed. And then I push her on her knees, and I pull my stupid cock out and fucking pee in the dripping viscera of her socket.

"I fucking hate the forest," I mumble to myself, somehow exhausted, and bring the bottle to my mouth, chugging the warm tequila. The shoelace tied around the neck of the bottle is resting on my face as I chug more and more of the tequila in big gulps. Big, big gulps, and it all goes down like peach tea. Ahh! Erik and Savage are staring at me like I just shat out a fucking tornado or something.

"Let's go," I say.

They give each other a look. Then—

Smash cut! It's dark and we are still in the forest, but the COLOURS have returned, and, holy shit, they are pretty. My goodness. Look at nature now! Ha ha ha! Erik walks up. I think I was dancing with a pine tree, but now I've stopped, and he puts his arm around me. "Should have drank from one of the other bottles. Why do you think I tied the shoelace on it? I put like two fluid ounces of LSD in that bottle. Maybe more. Get it? *Laced?*"

I look up into a nearby tree, and I see Savage impossibly standing on a branch. I think he's talking to an owl. Then he lights a firecracker and stuffs it into a crevice in the tree and jumps away onto another branch like some wild monkey or some shit. I point up at him and look at Erik.

Erik just waves it off. "There were a bunch of pterodactyls flying overhead, screeching and shit. It was scaring him, so I gave him a shitload of fireworks and told him to blow up their nests. It's fine. It's keeping him happy," he says, smiling, his eyes black like a shark's.

Erik throws some sticks and broken logs and bark and shit on the makeshift firepit. Things are coming to life now in so many ways, it's almost hard to process.

"Let's bring some tunes to this lonely forest!" a voice says.

"Good idea!" Erik says then goes into the Blunderbus to retrieve the gold-coloured ghetto blaster. He puts in the cassette and presses play. It's the album *Bricks Are Heavy* by L7. The song "Wargasm" roars out of the speakers, the music sounding so much more violent and intrusive being played in these dark woods. It's almost like we are daring *something* to reveal *itself* and come out of the darkness to press our stop button and shut us up.

Erik calls me Dylan—not the first time he's done this as of recently.

Erik then puts in a new cassette. It is the album commonly referred to as *Symbols* by German industrial band KMFDM. The song "Megalomaniac" plays as he takes a deep breath and begins TWIRLING his daisy chain of glow sticks. "On April twentieth, Eric Harris and Dylan Klebold, both wearing black trench coats, arrive at Columbine High School and begin their shooting rampage that will ROCK the entire world!" His TWIRLING gains speed and aggression.

"Harris is armed with a Hi-Point 995 Carbine, a Savage 67H pump-action shotgun, and two knives. He wears a white T-shirt with the words NATURAL SELECTION printed in BLACK.

"Klebold is armed with an Intratec TEC-DC9, a Stevens 311D double-barreled sawed-off shotgun, and two knives. He is wearing a black shirt with the word WRATH printed in RED.

"Rachel Scott, killed on the grass outside west entrance by Harris. Daniel Rohrbough, killed at the bottom of the stairs leading to west entrance by Harris. William David Sanders—he was the oldest victim at forty-seven years old. He was shot in the hallway near the library by Harris. Died of blood loss in a science classroom. Kyle Velasquez killed while sitting on a chair near the middle of the north computer table in the library by Klebold. Steven Curnow, youngest victim at age fourteen, killed at the west end of the south computer table in the library by Harris. Cassie Bernall, who believed in God, was killed while hiding under a library table by Harris. Isaiah Shoels, killed while hiding under a library table by Harris. Matthew Kechter, killed while hiding under a library table by Klebold. Lauren Townsend, killed while hiding under a library table by Klebold. John Tomlin, killed next to a library table by Klebold after being wounded by Harris. Kelly Fleming, killed next to a library table by Harris. Daniel Mauser, killed while hiding under a library table by Harris. Corey DePooter, killed while hiding under a library table by Klebold.

"Final tally: Harris 8, Klebold 5, for a total of 13 dead and 24 injured. Harris killed himself by firing his shotgun through the roof of his mouth. Klebold shot himself in his left temple with his TEC-9.

"The duo, also known as members of the Trench Coat Mafia, also brought explosives—none of which detonated properly and thus caused no major harm. Police said if the two twenty-pound propane bombs that they snuck into the cafeteria prior to their gunfire went off, that the death toll could have easily been in the thousands.

"The massacre began at 11:19 a.m. and ended at 12:08 p.m., MDT. Lasting a total of forty-nine minutes which, coincidentally, was the total length of *Adios*, the newest album by KMFDM, Harris and Klebold's favorite band. *Adios* was released on the same day of the Columbine High School Massacre: April 20, 1999."

Erik stops TWIRLING. "We can listen to *Adios* next if you want. I have that one too. I just chose *Symbols* because it was the shooters' favorite album. Not to mention the first song's referencing of wolves and pyracy."

Erik howls.

The song ends, and during the empty pause before the next one, we hear, far off in the distance, a distraught voice. Shrill and agitated but a man's voice, no doubt. It is muddled by the space and denseness of our stupid environment, thus making it hard to pinpoint exactly what they're screaming, but I pick up a prayerlike quality to the words. An aggressive desperation. I hit stop on the ghetto blaster right before, seemingly, the ribbon rolls onto the next song, and suddenly, the screamer's words get a cunt-hair more isolated, and the emotion being expressed becomes all the more real: fear. We stand still, quietly listening as the remote voice pleads with a force that clearly has power over him.

"He's bargaining with a captor," I whisper to Erik. "Didn't you say these woods are popular for gangland slayings?"

Erik burps, then gives a doubtful smile. "Who the fuck hangs around in the woods at night?" But before I can form my face into an *"are you fucking kidding me"* expression, Erik cups his hands over his mouth and shouts, "KILL THE STOOL PIGEON!"

"Erik, shut the fuck up!"

There's a quick succession of faraway gunshots as Erik resumes the music. The song "Stray Bullet" is now playing, and I'm morally certain Erik has lost his goddamn mind. Surely, the combination of high-grade psychedelics along with our recent dabbling into the supernatural is corrupting our minds. Even worse, our souls! He gives me a goofy look like *Oops! My bad!*

Then a moment later, Savage hollers at us from the branches. Somehow, he's in another tree and now much higher than the previous one I last saw him in. He's holding a giant puke-green egg. "I found breakfast!" he says, then throws the egg down, and it splats on my forehead.

*****

The boys detest the shows Friends, ER, Law and Order, The Simpsons, Who Wants to Be a Millionaire, Jerry Springer, Maury, *and most network television in general. However,* Dawson's Creek *on the WB is slowly becoming their favorite program.*

We declare the shopping cart the worst invention ever. We write a four-minute song about it, where we use the word "cunt" forty-seven times.

The boys disavow the book Tuesdays with Morrie. *They go to bookstores and sneak copies into the bathroom, where they smear their excrement on page 69. They return the books to the shelves. They have done this twenty-five times.*

We buy three cartons of menthol cigarettes, soak the filters in LSD, and leave packs in playgrounds all over the state.

The boys disavow the parents of the band Creed for not putting their babies in microwaves and engaging the defrost setting.

*****

We leave the Freetown State Forest the following morning, stopping at the first convenience store we find. We wrap up our midsections in beach towels and head inside to buy cigarettes and that caffeinated water we like, Crank 2-0. At the register, a "fuck me hard" blond hardbody twentysomething with a power smile asks us if we are nudists. There's a sign near the register that says if you weren't born before this date, we can't sell you cigs. The digital readout says

September 10, 1981, and in the parking lot, I scold Erik for making us lose the better part of a week to binge-tripping in the Bridgewater Triangle. He says it was an artistic pilgrimage and purposely drops his towel after saying this. Bear in mind, it's not even 9:00 a.m., and we're pumping gas alongside nine-to-five civilians.

Then Savage and Erik scour the Blunderbus for quarters.

Erik and Savage take turns using the payphone to chat with their dames. They ask if I want to talk to Becky, and I shake my head no. "Phone time is reserved for girlfriends and corralling a schmuck to bail you out of jail." And you can tell this makes them uneasy. Like I'm the weird wild animal for not wanting to willfully join the rest of my pack in the fucking zoo despite the amenities they claim you get for being fucking caged. Big fucking whoop.

They spend practically another fucking week chatting on the phone. I scream that we are going nowhere and it's their fault if we don't appear on TRL, and when they hang up, they tell me I'm ruining a good thing with Rebecca because I don't want to be happy. I tell them a relationship is essentially low-tier slavery but ultimately results in more back scars from constant whipping, and we get back in the Blunderbus and head to Rhode Island. And it is maybe an hour later when we are on the stretch of highway that's adjacent to that brand-new gargantuan mall in Providence. Savage screams and says he knows an artist friend who's planning on converting a section of the parking garage into an apartment, and he's doing this as a form of creative rebellion, but I am barely paying any mind. Instead, I am sitting in the way back, drawing erotic renderings of my muse and writing new songs that fucking pop pop pop.

Erik is sitting up front, accompanying Savage. He's doing whip-its one after another and getting "visions" that make him believe, quite steadfastly, that our band, our music, and all our doings are predestined, and the road we are taking—the literal road, I guess— has been set in motion eons ago. He says that the first domino that fell at the beginning of it all is employing the same energy that is consequently carrying us forward now. He says déjà vu is God telling you that the universe is a controlled demolition, and our lives are pieces of the debris, and they fall precisely how they are meant to.

He says this while passing the balloons to me and Savage, telling us to suck in the gas and to do this five or six times in rapid succession while limiting our oxygen absorption in between. He says if you do this, your eyesight will start getting wobbly, and this is usually indicative of when the visions will manifest themselves in what can only be called psychic phenomenon, and then the secrets to this particular dimension will be revealed as our conscious minds get launched to fucking Pluto.

At the show, after getting all set up, we're about to start jamming. And that's when some stagehand, a barely legal mall-goth, comes out to address whatever technical difficulty that has just arisen. So she's bending over at the front of the stage to check the fucking wires or whatever, and that's when there's a tap on my shoulder, and I turn, expecting one of the boys, but it's actually the Muse. She's looking ethereal and beautiful and slightly blurry, and she points at the mall-goth's black denim ass, and I waltz over and, with my boot, launch her headfirst right off the fucking stage! We laugh and she stands up looking like she just lost most of her goddamn marbles. The crowd of maybe two hundred people just erupt, emitting indomitable waves of energy that we volley right back to them. And, of course, the three of us are right away fucking dialed in! Right out of the gate. "Bride Burning" is the name of the first song we play, and I give an impromptu kick-ass solo as Erik chases the mall-goth around with a Zippo and an aerosol can.

Bride burning is a growing form of domestic abuse particular to Middle Eastern countries, where dowries to the groom are expected from the woman's family for the express purpose of incentivizing marriage to that particular woman. Bride burning is something of an open secret and is used to disguise outright murder as an accidental death or suicide. Cases have been on the rise, mostly in India, where a 1996 report from Indian police claimed that a newly married woman was set on fire roughly every ninety minutes that year.

After the show, the greasy owner of the club—some Wayne Newton lookalike with a pompadour and a track suit—invites us to his back office to give us stinging "attaboy" slaps on the back with his fucking Hamburger Helper hand. His name is Dom.

He says, "You boys did a fantastic job! The crowd here loves that lowbrow high-energy sociopathic shit! You boys are invited back anytime!"

He paid us an extra two hundred and even let us partake in his private stock of "EXCELLENT FUCKING COCAINE," what the boys and I call *Disco*. We go around the room, devouring lines. My first rail instantly numbs my NOSE, and I give a quick quiet prayer expressing gratitude on the power of drugs to free us from pain. I thank Dom, but he doesn't hear me. He's showing off his collection of throwing-knives that he insists we chuck at the faraway wall that's adorned with a collage of vintage election posters of RFK.

Erik says, "*Sirhan* me one of those knives." And Dom bursts into a wide-eyed screaming laugh that makes everything in close proximity rattle and shake so much that I immediately have to poo.

He directs me to his private bathroom, where there's dried droplets blood scattered all over the floor and sink. I make a point not to touch anything integral, and anything I do, I use Kleenex to wipe away any *trace evidence*.

"It's probably from a cocaine-induced nosebleed," Classic Nick says to himself in the mirror as he takes a deep breath and instantly has to take another shit.

When I come back, Savage is chatting up Dom, who's inserting a Rod Stewart CD into his stereo. "Young Turks" plays at low volume. Erik has a cigarette in his mouth, bee-bopping to the music and doing his own thing, as the Disco tends to make him somewhat introverted. Whenever we toot, we usually joke that a future coke binge will unintentionally make him release a solo album. He always editorializes the joke afterward, adding, "My cocaine music will be so good, they will give me a *Grammy*."

Get it? Grammy?

Savage is the opposite. Savage—who turns into a fucking blabbermouth when his nose gets powdered—is talking about a bootleg VHS of *American Beauty* that he has in the bus and how Dom should watch it and how it will surely dominate at the Oscars blah blah blah, and how it's a good family movie, and he could watch it with his wife and kids.

Savage snorts and rubs his nose. "Do you have any kids, Dom?"

Dom snorts a line, then takes a moment to process the power it carries. "Oh sure. One daughter, nineteen. She's the one youse boys were tormenting on stage out there," he says in a serious tone.

And as Dom leans down to take another hit, Erik and I, one after the other, give Savage a smack to the side of his gorilla head as a "*look what you just did*" response, but also to start getting Savage's blood up in case we need his simian prowess to avoid any sort of "whackings" that may or may not be forthcoming from Big Dom here.

Dom lifts his head, then stands erect, and he's now flashing a mean mug, and he's slowly approaching us, lumbering his girthy frame toward us. And I take note that all the throwing knives are currently in JFK's face and abdomen, sticking out of the wall.

Then a flash of gold! And out of nowhere, Dom's got a fucking gun in his hand. No doubt custom-made gold-plated, and I instantly know in my heart of hearts this gun has a history, sordid and all. He raises it up to brain level at the same time Erik chuckles and points around the office. "Look, soundproofing. What do you know?"

Then Dom pulls the trigger.

Click!

Dom bursts into hysterics. "Boys! I'm only fucking with youse! I ain't gonna shoot youse after you made me so much money tonight! Fucking guys! I know one of youse defecated in your drawers as I am picking up the faint whiff of scared shit."

Savage raises his hand. "Sorry about that."

Dom gives us a bear hug, and we do another line of Disco that I barely feel since my adrenaline is already jacked.

"So that wasn't your daughter?" Erik says, rubbing some Disco all over his gums.

"Oh no. She is! Pride and joy and all that shit, but fuck her. That dumb twat says she's voting for Al Gore come November, which serves me right, I guess, for sending her to RISD."

*****

We peel out of the parking lot blaring "The Ballad of Buckethead," the first track on Erik's mixtape he just put in. Savage is drinking tequila, navigating by way of the few signs the city still has that aren't missing or knocked down or bent over, trying to find the on-ramp to head back onto the I-95 to go back to the Bay State for our next gig, a fucking Sunday show in New Bedford.

Erik "drops anchor" (it's actually two seventy-pound dumbbells we stole from the gym that we call our anchor!), which means he ties the rope around his midsection to prevent being thrown overboard, which is precisely the reason you should acquire a vehicular anchor if you're ever planning on doing any car surfing on top of a special-needs bus. Safety first, folks! We are not savages here.

Erik pops out of the ceiling's emergency exit and sits on the roof of the Blunderbus. I pass him the megaphone, and he starts to sing along with his playlist. It's karaoke by way of drive-by as Erik accosts both motorized and pedestrian passersby with amplified lyricism.

And seriously, fuck Erik. His voice really isn't that bad. Not bad at all.

So Erik has the long shiny black rock and roll hair. Think Peter Steele. The abs. The sinewy musculature that he calls his "Bruce Lee striations." This asshole just picked up the piano willy-nilly one winter and learned it—kind of mastered it, really, but don't tell him I said that! The jerk-off probably has all sorts of instruments in him just waiting to purge and express themselves. I swear to gawd, I'm certain the Muse is a sadist. Don't tell her I said that!

It certainly feels unfair, I guess. But at the end of the day, you have to respect talent even when it's raw (like real RAW), no matter how unfair to the musically disciplined for the reason that I had to earn my goddamn shredding abilities through repeated practice and many gawd damn days of social isolation.

The next songs on the mixtape are "Working Class Whore" by Pulley then "Dreaming Black Neon" by Nevermore followed by "Cassius 1999" by Cassius. The whole time, Erik is on the roof, holding tight, singing along, and belting out the words through the megaphone—which, for the record, has a modest strap off the handle that you can secure around your wrist so everybody and everything is secure.

I yell to Savage, "Do you think you're getting close to the freeway?"

He sips from the bottle, corks it, and tosses it back to me. "Nope!"

"Do any of these streets look familiar?" I ask, then take a healthy swig of tequila.

He clears his throat. "I'm not going to lie, Class. I am pretty sure that Disco we just tooted reignited all that LSD we are just coming off from."

"Oh! that makes sense." I look to the back of the bus and see the ghosts of Mark Sandman and Stanley Kubrick sitting quietly on the same bench. "Yup. A lot of sense."

Erik pops his head straight down from the roof, and I'm not entirely sure how he's managing to do this maneuver. Whatever. "Savage! You do realize you've been doing circles around downtown, right?"

Savage screams (or maybe it's a moan), "Ah shit!" Then he ejects Erik's mixtape. "I can't fucking concentrate with your music," he shouts, opening the door and chucking the tape outside. "Out ya go!"

"Nooo!" Erik screams, now with the megaphone.

"It's about time we play my fucking music," Savage says. Producing a cassette out of seemingly nowhere, he inserts it into the ghetto blaster. "I Need Adventure" by GG Allin plays. I hand him the bottle, and he screams "LET'S FUCK THIS PIG!" as he begins to accelerate while downing some tequila.

"Goddammit, Savage. You're tripping balls still! You can't fucking see! We can just park the bus and wait it out till tomorrow!"

"I'll help ya navigate, buddy!" Erik is still shouting into the cab of the Blunderbus with the megaphone. "I'll just have to get closer!"

"This isn't necessary—" I stop myself midsentence. What the fuck am I doing? They're not going to fucking listen to me, and the moment I sit down and have this realization, the rope tethered to Erik's waist goes slack, then drops in a pile unto itself in the aisle between the bus's benched seats. Erik's head reemerges in the opening in the ceiling. He looks at me and gives me an earnest salute like he's a fucking hero, which I pooh-pooh with a low-energy hand gesture and make raspberries with my tongue.

Erik's focus shifts to somewhere behind me as he points. "Sandman! No fucking way!" Erik then somehow makes dual hand horns and sticks out his tongue. "Was sorry to hear about your passing, bro! You're a personal hero! *Like Swimming* belongs under museum glass!"

Classic Nick, with a look that denotes extreme confusion, turns to the back of the bus. Maybe he mumbles "The fuck?" or "No shit?" to himself or something similar to express his uncertainty about his current placement in life and all these wild things that have been happening this summer.

He pooh-poohs again. Just enjoy the ride, Class, *he thinks to himself.* After all, you play crazy games, you win crazy prizes.

Erik gives a much shyer acknowledging of the other apparition sitting in the back of the special-needs bus. "Mr. Kubrick. Thank you for *The Shining*."

Erik's head disappears. There's a hasty procession of loud stomping ushering toward the front of the bus in hard denting sounds that echo in that hollow metallic way, and the whole thing seems to be doubling the tension with every beat. Think of a drummer banging away on the snare drum and the visceral suspense that generates within your pulse. And then there's a pause, a break. That's where he then leaps off the roof and lands on top of the modest hood with a deep crunch that reverberates throughout the entirety of the vessel. The inevitable bashing of the crash cymbal(s).

Erik takes a moment to stabilize himself, death grips on the wiper blades and the top of the hood, and tucking up his feet to an actionable position. All the while, the megaphone is still tethered to his arm. He lets out a war cry celebrating his accomplishments. "Ahhhhh!" He looks around at his surroundings, takes ahold of the megaphone. But when his focus finally settles on Savage, Erik's expression instantly shifts, and his scowling face emerges. He brings the bullhorn to his mouth. "Wake the fuck up! Are you fucking kidding me?"

"I was just resting my eyes," Savage says sheepishly.

"Asshole! You are driving a bus!" Erik's amplified voice is still penetrating amidst a continuous gust and behind the laminated glass of the bus's windscreen.

Savage's eyes get narrow. "Fine! You don't like the way I operate a motor vehicle? Then how about I park this bastard!"

"Bruise Violet" by Babes in Toyland plays next off Savage's mixtape.

Meanwhile, in the back, Classic Nick—having broken out the tequila bottle with the shoelace about a minute prior—generously adds another squirt or four of LSD on account of wanting to be as fucked up as humanly possible when they inevitably crash and die or get arrested. He is thinking, Who the hell wants to suffer the consequences to their actions while being sober? *And with that thought, he cheer'd the bottle to his unseen companions.*

The ghosts demand a toast, and it just so happens that when I stand to give it, I feel the warm moist lips of the Muse softly peck on my cheek. Mark and Stanley nod understandingly, and it is on.

I clear my throat. "Fuck cause and effect and all the tax they collect. Fuck law and order and any current psychiatric disorder. Fuck Bethlehem, fuck Mecca, and fuck that dumb bitch named Rebecca. Fuck punk, fuck rock, and when you do, you use your cock! Fuck luck, fuck strife because we are all Fuck'd for Life. Fuck sin and fuck morality. But most of all, fuck reality!"

Mark and Stanley give a silent applause as I chug from the laced bottle for a solid five seconds.

It's at that moment Classic Nick hears Savage scream at Erik, still threatening to stop the bus. He gives an incredulous nostril snort, shrugging his shoulders. "What a concept, huh?"

Erik screams, "I'm trying to help you! I am risking my life to help you navigate, you ungrateful fucking gorilla! Now turn on your headlights!" He looks around. "I think we are near the performing arts center!"

Savage engages the switch for the headlamps, night, and day. "Jesus! This makes shit so much easier!" He points at the road. "Erik, what's that?"

Erik turns to look as Savage slams on the brakes. Erik goes flying off the hood and lands like a bowling pin, tumbling on the pavement. Savage is dazed, nonplussed, he begins blinking a lot and, absentmindedly, he initiates the control to the small stop sign on the side of the bus that then extends outward, and a binary set of amber lights start to flash.

I prance to the front of the bus, and I don't know why exactly. "Why did you stop so suddenly?"

Savage points to the street. "Owen Hart is in standing in the middle of the road. Look! Do you see him too? Please tell me you also see him."

"I don't know," I mumble, pretending I don't see the dead wrestler waving at us. I try to think of something noncommittal to say. "So…antisemitism is bad, huh?"

Savage turns his head to look at me. He does this very quickly. *"WHAT!"*

"Want some more tequila?" I ask, holding out the bottle. "I put more butter in it!"

Savage erupts. "Okay! Time out! What the hell is going on with this fucking LSD?"

"Hey, guys!" Erik says, looking all stiff and unmovable like a cheap discarded action fiction. He's still lying in the street. He's speaking into the megaphone—which, surprisingly, didn't break, although holding it looks like it is causing him a considerable amount of pain.

We step outside. "Heeeey, buddy. How's my favorite bass player doing?" I ask, affecting a tone similar to the one I used to use when talking to my last living great-grandfather, a man who looked like a frog and a thousand-year-old skin tag had a baby.

"Any chance you guys can call a bone surgeon or someone with a PhD in organ science? Maybe someone to check to see if I have any internal bleeding? Please and thank you? I can feel my soul uncoupling from my body as we speak."

Back inside the bus, "Chaos Theory" by the Dead Milkmen starts playing.

I hold out the bottle. "Want some tequila? It's extra heavy on the shoelace, if you catch my drift."

"Yeah. Okay," Erik says dryly as he sits upright with slow methodical movements like a slasher-film antagonist coming back to life.

Next Chapter

The triage nurse at the emergency room says to Erik that his pupils are quite large, and he replies, "All the better to see you with, my dear." And this sends Savage and me over the fucking edge with animated hysterics.

I jump up on a table, unbutton the butt flap to my onesie, rest my ass cheeks against the front desk's window, and moon all the patients waiting in the lobby. I turn around to see their reactions, and somehow, Savage is over there! I knock on the glass, pointing and laughing. When he looks back at me, I gesture like, *"How the hell you get out there so fast?"* But he's ripping and tossing pages out of the shitty magazines. He then prances back over to us in triage real silly like.

Erik's eyes go wonky, and he pukes on the nurse. Savage and me stick out our tongues and do hand-horns and belt out an unrehearsed heavy metal iteration of "Hospital Food" by Eels. That's when this cunt signals over a couple security dudes. She steps out to talk to them, and I immediately notice the leader of the two security guards has CAT EYES. And as he responds to the nurse, he speaks in linguistic black magic. Veiled enchantments—the logistics of which I can only describe as verbal BACKWARD MASKING.

Savage whispers in my ear, "He's definitely a warlock." And I affirm his assessment with a solemn nod.

I have no goddamn idea what monotone spells he's attempting to conjure up, but I know for sure his *perceived voice*—the tone and cadence he wants people to hear—was as artificial as the plastic dog poop you can buy for pranking your stepmother by putting it in her sock drawer, which nonetheless smelled as awful as the real shit. I may have actually said this aloud. I'm not sure. I was paying attention to his initial dialogue but then refocused on the hospital's overhead lights, which are humming and shaking and doing that weird superfast flickering thing that fluorescent lights do. Then the COLOURS suddenly evaporate as I feel the LSD begin to turn on me.

Before he has a chance to say anything to me, I tell Cat Eyes to shut up, then point up to the fluorescents. "This shit lighting is activating my latent serial-killer genes. Best we turn them off before things get hairy, yeah?"

He studies my face. "Oh, all you guys' eyes are dilated?" he says, looking back to the triage nurse. He turns back to me. "What are you boys on? You can tell us. You are in a safe place."

Savage says to me, "Let me handle this," then turns to the guards. "Listen, warlocks. We just came out of the spooky woods where we were camping for days in our special-needs bus, drinking so much shoelace." He pauses to laugh, then looks at me, and I flash him a *what the hell are you saying?* look. He shrugs, turns back to Cat Eyes. "It's like a cursed triangle. There are aliens and Pukwudgies and pterodactyls—"

"They are actually Thunderbirds," I whisper in his ear, and for a second, he looks heartbroken. I add a nod, affirming the veracity of my interjection. "Sorry, bud."

"Whatever. I was destroying their nests with crack—"

The guards' faces flash concern.

"Firecrackers. Oh! And we also just destroyed the last hospital we were at. It was a lunatic asylum. The roofing collapsed, but we managed to get out safe."

I can't help but laugh. "What the fuck, man? Stop talking! Stop saying words! Why are you saying all this? This sounds so bad!"

Savage admonishes me, "It's the truth!"

Hearing that makes me pause a moment and reflect on the utter horror of his last statement. *Oh shit!*

I look at the guards and burst out in a laugh. "Fuck it! Yeah, that's 100 percent correct. We did all those things."

The guards are staring at us in shock, just blinking. "Anything else?" Cat Eyes says just as Erik's eyes roll back in their sockets, and he slumps backward on the bed, losing consciousness.

The nurse calls for assistance when he starts seizing. The response is almost instantaneous as two more medical professionals burst into the modest space, almost like they were behind the door waiting to be summoned. Hospital jargon like magic spells being cast with terms such as "CCs" and "vitals" and "internal bleeding" and "massive cranial trauma" are urgently volleyed between the players in green scrubs.

Savage and I try explaining to them that he's just doing this for attention, that he loves it when people fuss over him. That's when the lady doctor with the penetrating eyes tells the nurse to "get these idiots out of here." And so she ushers the four of us out of the doorway of the triage unit into the hallway adjacent to the lobby. I try telling her to jam a couple of her lady fingers in his ass to stimulate his prostate and how he loves it when the dames engage his BUTT-on and that he'll surely snap out of it then, but she scoffs and slams the door in my face midsentence.

I look at Savage and the guards. "I think I could be a doctor. Doesn't seem that hard."

"What the hell happened to your buddy in there, huh?" Cat Eyes asks suspiciously, like he's some slick gumshoe committed to NAILING his perp.

That's when I recall a realization Erik made years ago: how rent-a-cops are usually more dangerous than actual cops and that the worst security guard takes his job more seriously than the best police officer.

Savage is gesturing behind him. "He was car surfing on top of our sped bus. I hit the brakes when I saw Owen Hart standing in the road."

Cat Eyes's brow emotes curiosity. "The wrestler? The *dead* wrestler?"

Savage chuckles nervously. "I think our time in the triangle—"

"That's the haunted triangle, right?"

Savage smiles appreciatively. "Yeah, that's right. And I know what you're thinking. That our time in the spooky triangle probably left us with some residual spookiness, which will probably linger for a few days. But we've been dealing with a fair amount of SUPERNAT-

URE for some time now. Way before stepping one foot into the damn Indian burial swamp."

Fuck it, *Classic Nick thinks to himself.* Everyone is a potential fan, and everyone likes hearing stories about the crazy antics of rockers. Let's see how milquetoast these plastic badges actually are.

I nod. "Take last month, for example. Not getting into too many details, we did see the face of the Boss."

"Who's *the Boss*?"

"Judith Light! Tony Danza!" Savage and I shout as quickly as possible, yet we both manage to answer at the exact same time. Laughing, we turn to each other to high-five. "Now *that* was a great show! I mean, I don't know if it's art, but I like it."

"The moon," Savage says, clarifying. "We call him *the Boss* because he revealed his real face to us. And again, without going into too many details, we carry out tasks he gives to us."

"He transmits pure universal knowledge to us by way of moonbeams," I say, putting a cigarette in my mouth. And as I pat myself, checking for a lighter, Cat Eyes snatches the cigarette and crushes it in his hand. Then he wags his long index finger, gesturing *NO*.

"Jesus, either play with a ball of yarn or trim your nails, pal," I say in a defeated tone.

There's a noise behind us, a throat clearing. "Taking orders from an anthropomorphized celestial body, you say?"

Savage and I turn around to see a short bald man with a tragically studious face complete with a diminished chin and glasses like hockey pucks that start to fog up when he blows on his coffee. He's wearing a corduroy jacket with elbow patches, and right away, we assume psychiatrist. And from the initial impression, we assume he's probably viciously brilliant along with, most likely, being highly respected within his field. We assume this partly due to a general disheveled air about him that suggests *quiet obsession*. Nothing too risqué, of course. But looking at him, you certainly can tell he's a man that prefers the abstract and cerebral over anything remotely real world, if there even is such a thing.

Not saying he's a bum or anything. He's certainly not as unkempt as us. At this point, we are practically feral. I mean, for

Chrissakes, I have a broken nose and raccoon eyes that I've had for weeks now and no goddamn memory of how that happened! Most of my clothing has holes, rips, missing buttons, scorch marks, and/or bloodstains. A couple months ago, I was asked to leave the bank because one of my shoes was slightly smoldering, and the smoke was burning the branch manager's eyes.

And then there's Savage, who has fucking safety pins pierced all down his outer ear. Maybe six or seven on each side, and a few of them look pretty infected. That was something we just did to him for shits and giggles while the gorilla was driving. There was almost a kind of sport to it. Anyway, Savage, the ape, was sexually assaulted a shitload as a kid, so he's got a pretty decent threshold for pain. Erik once smashed a whisky bottle over his head while he was sleeping, and he didn't even wake up!

Hard to remember when we pierced his ears. I know we had found the safety pins scattered throughout the parking lot of a boarded-up church and decided to surprise him with a new look while he was driving. Maybe we were drunk and acidic? Fuck knows anymore. All I know for sure is we definitely were not sober.

We are never sober.

Headshrinker is now drinking the steaming coffee out of a Styrofoam cup, practically chugging it. I assume he's hungover, but who the hell knows. I should probably stop assuming everyone else is also an alcoholic. It could just be something as innocent as exhaustion from working a nineteen-hour shift or something. When the cup is empty, he holds it between his teeth as he scribbles something down on a clipboard, and there's a weird pocket of silence that makes everything momentarily awkward, and I cannot help but think it is intentional. Headshrinkers like this bald fuck probably employ a whole slew of mind games that he weaponizes against all those he views as *less than*. Subtle psychological attacks launched at the unwitting, his petty way of punishing others for his OBVIOUS lack of sexual encounters. But hey, at least he has a clipboard.

A nurse approaches. She takes the empty cup out of his mouth. He stops his writing, and she hands him a new cup of hot coffee that he immediately starts to gulp.

"Let it cool down, Doctor," she says, putting a calming hand on his shoulder.

He ignores the advice, finishing the coffee in one go, and he gives her back the cup. "Another one?"

"Please," he says in hurried tone. "Brew another pot as soon as you can. I don't want what's-her-name making it. She makes it too weak."

She smiles warmly. "I'll be happy to if you promise you will eat something sooner rather than later. I can get you something out of the vending machine if you'd like. Chocolate bar?"

He nods his head. The nurse smiles once more before strolling off.

He turns back to us, his uninterested eyes magnified by the ridiculous thickness of his frames. There's a blankness to his gaze, as if he forgot where he was. He clears his throat. "Oh, that's right. Okay, gentlemen. At this point, I'm going to ask you to *voluntarily* come with me upstairs, where you will be admitted to the psychiatric ward."

Savage and I turn around, but Cat Eyes and his goon have closed in on us. There's a feeling of VIOLENT ANTICIPATION hanging in the air, and I think everyone in the vicinity can sense it.

I belch. "Yeah, that's not going to happen, headshrinker. We just came to get our friend checked out after he got his bell rung. He's the patient, not us. Not to mention, he doesn't even need a shrink. He probably just has a concussion and some bumps and bruises. No big deal. He'll be back to his normal frustrating self in no time. I am sure of it."

Headshrinker jots down a quick something, then looks back up. "If you volunteer admission, I can promise, as long as you pose no danger to yourselves or others, you will be released after the compulsory seventy-two hours. You have my word."

Savage scoffs, "And if we tell you to kiss our asses, what happens then?"

After he says this, the security guards move in a fraction closer— so close we can almost tell if they are circumcised or not.

Headshrinker focuses on me. "If you make me section you, I can keep you here indefinitely. Police report has already been filed on you boys."

"Police report!" I exclaim. "We didn't encounter any piggies. Besides, we drove ourselves here!"

"From my understanding, there are multiple witnesses to your collective…*episode*. Not to mention footage from a local WPRI news crew that, again, from what I was told, captured a significant portion of your—"

"Episode?" I say, cutting him off.

"That's right. But the police would rather see you boys get help for what all indicators clearly point to signs of ACUTE PSYCHOSIS. Which is nothing to be ashamed about. Around 25 percent of adults experience symptoms of psychosis at least once in their lifetime. The police would rather you fellas get treated than have to throw the book at you. But do realize, in here, I have the final authority. However, it does take a considerable amount of paperwork, and so I am asking as both a favor to me and you. Admit yourselves voluntarily, and if for three days, you boys can get along without incident while we assess your states of mind, I promise you will be released without a hitch and with no legal ramifications."

He jabs the clipboard with his finger for emphasis. "Make no mistake, gentlemen. *This* is what MERCY looks like."

"It has to be all three of us?"

The nurse returns with another coffee that he eagerly accepts. "Afraid so, boys. The three of you for three days."

I step forward, closer to the headshrinker, and you can feel the uptick in baseline tension when I do this. Quick gasps, constricting irises, and a hastening pulse. Every physiological marker on fucking standby. After all, a decent cross section of the people from Providence—police, local news, fellow commuters, not to mention these good people here at whatever old Puritan or Quaker this shithole is named after—they all seem to think we are unstable. Actual lunatics with time bombs in our coconuts. And who knows? Maybe they are right.

In an intimate whisper, I say to the headshrinker, "I want you to know I agree with your terms."

Headshrinker releases a deep sigh. "Really?"

"It stung hearing you be so matter-of-fact. But in the end, it's what I needed to hear. This is an act of mercy, and on behalf of me and my friends, I humbly thank you," I say, extending my hand, which he approaches reluctantly but eventually shakes.

Headshrinker smiles and it's obvious his face isn't used to going in that direction. "I have to say, this comes as a relief."

"Oh? Why do you say that?"

He looks around the room, making sure no one can hear. Then he leans in. "Because you boys are fucking maniacs!" he says, bursting out in what you could call a RUSTY LAUGH. But regardless, I can't help but yield to the humor and laugh along with him. "You're intimidating."

"Oh, now you're just pulling my leg!" I say, chuckling.

"I'm serious. You boys come off as quite intense, if I am being honest. I am look youse! You're dressed like bones from hell!" He leans in again, now employing a heavy whisper through the side of his mouth. "And if I am being real honest, I've been doing this job a long time. I've seen my fair share of the mentally divergent. And yeah, you boys are maniacs, but there's something else about youse. It's in your eyes."

"Signs of chronic alcohol and drug use?"

He laughs and slaps my arm. "Well, there's *that*, sure. That's obvious. But I am talking deeper. You boys are almost making a game out of your pathologies. If this was a TV show, you boys would be described as meta. You know what I am saying? It's like you guys are crazy not because of genetics or circumstance but because you *choose* to be. Almost as if there's a philosophy at play here."

I shake his hand again. "You're a smart man."

"And you as well. Both of you. And probably your long-haired friend too, although as of right now..." He blows raspberries as he gestures his thumb down. "It is not currently on full display. Let's just put it that way."

I laugh hard at that one, and his face brightens like nothing he's said has ever been thought of as funny before.

And when the laughter simmers down, he tosses back the coffee, then checks his watch. "So anyway, your friend is going to stay down here for probably another day or so, just for observation. But he should be fine. I, however, need to use the bathroom." He shakes the cup. "You only rent the stuff, yeah?" We give a quick chuckle, then he clears his throat. "But these young bucks," he says, using the clipboard to point to the security guards, "will be more than happy to lead you and your large friend upstairs to the psychiatric ward, where I will be with you momentarily."

We look each other in the eye and shake hands. I walk two paces away. "Oh shit." I quick snap my thumb! *DARN IT!* "Oh shit!" I project my voice a notch louder. "Excuse me! Dr. Zeus!" Now I am even putting a little texture into my voice. "Any chance you'll give us a fifteen-minute reprieve to smoke a cigarette and grab a few things from the bus? Some books for Erik. Savage's fiddle. Hell, if you let us bring our ACOUSTICS, we'd even be happy to play music each day for the other patients."

*****

In reference to Dom.
"We even have a shitload of *granita*, boys. On our last gig, the owner, he hooked us up with works last night! That was a great venue." I yawn. "What do you think?" I look to Savage. "Definitely play there again soon? He liked us!"

Savage yawns. "OH YEAH." His voice cracks so he clears his throat. "FOR SURE." He hocks a loogie. Spits.

"Did you say you have a shitload of granita?" Cat Eyes asks, except he's not really Cat Eyes anymore. We're in the sun now, the parking lot. "Is that similar to Italian ice?"

His subordinate is Devin, and his name is Dustin. *Wah wa wah waaaaa!* And even though he doesn't have *cat eyes*, wasn't "Cat Eyes" so much better than fucking "Dustin"?

"Yes, of course, Dustin."

Dustin asks, "'Yes, of course, to which question? Wait. What's your name, bearded man?"

Classic Nick dodges the question.

"Yes to both questions," I say.

"You really have Italian ice?"

Savage yawns. "It's not Italian ice. It's granita. But yes, Devin."

"Seriously, what's your name, man?"

"And you are going to give us some of this Italian ice?"

"My legal name is…" I yawn harder. "Classic Nick."

"It is not Italian ice, Devin. It is granita, but yes. Granita all around, man. Go crazy!"

Now they are all inside the Blunderbus. Savage opens a red cooler.

"Why *do you* have so much Italian ice?"

"I already explained that it's NOT ITALIAN ICE, Devin. It is granita." Savage slumps onto the nearest bus bench. He rubs his eyes. "Please keep up, yeah?"

The percussionist.

"What do you mean *threw in Italian ice?*"

"Goddammit…Devin." Savage isn't yawning now. "I fucking explained this…ALREADY." He's growling his words out like a poisonous whisper. "I…fucking ALREADY explained this." He's pounding the back of the bus bench, and at the same time, he pauses between certain words, emphasizing the word by itself or a sentence fragment. "After paying our fee…he offered to throw in a few extra hundred dollars… But instead, we wanted FUCKING GRANITA… We've heard from other bands that have played there before about how amazing his homemade granita is…and how when WE play there, how we HAVE TO ask for some granita to go. The owner agreed…Devin! He fucking agreed to give us granita!" He finishes by bashing the bench in front of him like he would a crash cymbal.

The vocals.

"Seriously though! What's your legal name? As it appears on your license?"

I show Dustin my license. "CLASSIC NICK! CLASSIC NICK! DEVIN, YOU FUCKING CUNT! READ THE FUCKING WORDS, YOU FUCK-ING PIGEON!" I scream.

At the end of the day, if we are out of our element and lost amongst a newly unveiled world of strange light, shadows, eccentric people, we must always try to remember to trail back to what we are familiar with so we have something CONSTANT *to hold on to. Something* REAL.

While Devin and Dustin sit down on bench seating across the aisle from each other, eating granita, Savage puts on a cassette. The album is *Daydream Nation*. "Eric's Trip" plays. Then under the pretense of "helping him find some things," he takes me aside. "Are you fucking sure they are not warlocks? They are driving me insane." He puts his hand flat to his head, indicating the level he is at. "INSANE!"

I look around. I probably look like quite the fucking sight right now. All beaten down, post-drunk, post-popped, and rock and roll dirty. "I think this is just how average SHEEP behave?"

"They talk about nothing! Nothing at all!" he says in a shouting whisper, careful not to hip the two wankers to what he's saying. "And the one or two things they talk about is ALL THEY FUCKING TALK ABOUT!"

"I hear you, man. I am just saying. I think this is just an average conversation from a day walker. Living in the sunlight, every day, makes everything sterile."

From the other end of the bus, there's a bit of stirring. Savage and Classic Nick brace themselves for more verbal diarrhea.

Dustin wipes off the corner of his mouth. "You think we can turn down this music to a polite volume? Maybe take some of these skull-and-crossbones flags down and let in some light?"

"I agree," Devin says with a mouthful. He then asks, "Where did you guys say you got this Italian ice from again?"

Savage, with a clenched jaw through gritted teeth, let's out a mumble of profanities.

"What the hell are you guys listening to?"

"Sonic Youth."

"It's weird. Can you put something else on?"

"No."

"Do you have any Staind?"

Savage flashes a look at me that I know means he wants to kill them. "We…don't…listen…to…them. We…have…self-respect. We…are…not…animals."

Devin chuckles. "You guys probably like Creed though. I mean, who doesn't love Creed? They are excellent."

Savage sits down on a bench in the back, waits a moment, then starts slamming his face into the seat in front of him. He does this over and over and over and over again as the song "Providence" starts playing?

"What is this?"

In an exasperated tone, he replies, "I don't know anymore. Hell?" He's so defeated, he tosses his fiddle aside, choosing not to bring it. Nothing can bring him any joy now.

"No, butthead," Devin says in a Frat Boy cadence. "What's this?" he asks, holding up a copy of *Man into Wolf* by Robert Eisler.

"It's a book goddammit! You never read a book before?"

"Why are you guys slowing down?"

"Fucking sun!" Savage and I, exiting the Blunderbus with cigarettes in our mouths, hoist the straps of our bags onto our shoulders. We yawn at the same time, both of us dropping our cigarettes. "Because it's getting late."

"Ungodly hour."

Languidly, they begin walking back through the fucking parking lot.

"It's not even seven thirty in the morning."

I rub my head. Savage groans. *Parking lots are mechanical seas where all the mirrors and glare off the cars' bodies are like a thousand sentient daggers that specifically target the goddamn eyeballs.*

"This is the time the *normal* are awake."

I groan.

Savage uses his big paw to shield his eyes from the sun. "We never claimed to be normal."

"All over the world. Every day. This is how the world functions."

"All over the world!" Devin repeats.

"Fuck the world."

They get back to the hospital through the automatic doors back into the lobby. Savage and Classic Nick drop their bags to rub their eyes, happy at last to be out of the god-awful sunlight.

"Humans are born to follow a circadian rhythm. Factory settings. Out of the box!"

Savage screams, "How about this, huh? Fuck your box! Fuck your factory! And neither of youse have any fucking rhythm! Okay! You're both fucking boring!"

I step in front of Savage, standing face-to-face with the guards, and add, "And who the fuck said we are human?"

$$*****$$

Two minutes later, Classic Nick is holding back Savage, or at least Savage is listening to what he has to say and not going into full-on berserker mode. Not that Savage aims to do any harm to Classic Nick. Not at all. Just those "smug cunts."

Classic Nick says, "Okay, big boy. Are you going to play nice? These kind folks here want to help us. They seem to think we're a bit MOONSTRUCK *but feel confident that a short stay here—an extended weekend, essentially—would do us good at this point. I'd think we'd be fools for turning down their offer. Damn fools!" He leans in, whispering in the gorilla's ear, "It's the sunlight, Savage. I promise! We are not used to it, so it is fucking with our heads. That's all."*

"They have fucking GOAT EYES now," Savage says, all wide-eyed. "Both of them! I am telling you, they are fucking warlocks! You see it, don't you?"

"I am telling you, buddy. It is all in your head."

"Of course it is, *buddy*!" Dustin says, holding up the squirt bottle of LSD—our squirt bottle of LSD! He must have snagged it when he was in the Blunderbus, when we weren't looking. "'It's all in your head. That's one hell of an understatement. And judging by you guy's behavior and the levels of this shit the doctors say are present in your friend's bloodwork, I am guessing there's a lot more going on in all your heads. More than you even realize." When he laughs, he laughs like a pervert.

The triage nurse comes up and takes the LSD from Special Agent Dustin, putting it in a clear medical ziplock baggie. Then with a marker, she scribbles some black magic on the blank label. When she's finished, she hands it to an orderly. "Send this to the lab."

I stare at both guards. "You plundered from *us*?"

They laugh and high-five. "I guess we did!"

"You came onto *our* PYRATE ship, and you took from *our* stock. Is *that* what *you* are saying?"

"That's right," Dustin says, snapping his fingers like *gotcha!* And when he does this, his eyes get weird. His pupils contort and turn into demonic rectangles. "What the hell are *youse* going to do about it?"

A double door without knobs or handles opens, and—one, two, three, *four*—more security guards enter the lobby. They are wearing shit similar to riot gear, I guess. They split into groups of two, lowering their face shields as the division occurs.

Classic Nick scratches his head. Okay?

Devin chuckles. He too has goat eyes now. "That's right, boys. Looks like we are the real pyrates since we took your booty."

I turn to Savage and slap him on the shoulder. "All right, pal. I made a mistake here. Please and thank you, get us the fuck out of here!"

Berserker mode activated!

I do a quick scan around the emergency ward, immediately noticing how we are suddenly the center of attention as all eyes are now focusing intently on us. Everyone is watching. It's funny. Everywhere we go, we cultivate an audience. Maybe some people are just born to create stages everywhere they stand.

"AVAST, people! We are the real fucking PYRATES! Real deal and highly trained! Do not believe these jokers. They are FALSE PYRATES, and once we RECLAIM our BOOTY, we will free our MATEY who, as of right now, remains your CAPTIVE. And from there, we will BURN DOWN THIS INSTITUTION." Savage is screaming this as he does some frantic stirring motions with his hands, which I'm not sure why or what he was going for exactly.

Devin says, "This is just an episode, fellas. You guys are having a psychotic break!"

"Sure, we're psychotic! But PYRATES."

Dustin pauses. "'Psychotic *BUTT PYRATES*!'" He's bursting with hysterics. His goat eyes are crying now. He looks to Devin, who's red in the face and overcome by a fit of laughter and coughing.

"That's not what I meant." I get louder. "I was going to say 'nonetheless.' We are psychotic but pyrates…"

And I said it again! I just fucking doubled down on that one. How the fuck does that happen?

Everyone here is getting their money's worth today. Across the lobby, there's a janitor chuckling. All the patients are chortling and pointing at me. The four guards in face shields are still in hysterics. Dustin is bent over, using the console people use to sign in to support himself. Devin signals that they need a moment.

Even the triage nurse, despite her obvious restraint, can't help but crack up.

"You pieces of shit!" I say, waltzing over to the nearest bank of chairs and grabbing the hat off the head of some college dude sitting in the lobby. The college kid stops giggling and immediately begins to protest/bitch/cry/complain. Fucking predictable! I turn around real quick, get a cunt hair away from his face, lock eyes with him, bare my teeth, and emit the gnarliest low-growl you ever fucking heard in the wild, let alone an emergency ward in Rhode Island. That shuts him up.

I look at the hat. "Hmmm. Providence Bruins, no shit?" I say, giving him a thumbs-up, and it is quite apparent he has no idea how to respond.

I frisbee the hat, hitting Devin with the flat brim right on the bridge of his nose. He screams. "Ow!"

I stand straight, feet planted firmly on the linoleum. "You fucking sheep have no fucking idea I have an actual NUCLEAR FUCKING WARHEAD for a soul!"

"We shit MUSHROOM CLOUDS every day!" Savage says. Then during the tense moment, he pauses to point at me. "Hey! Tattoo idea. Mushroom clouds on our backs?"

"Not bad," I say, digging the idea. I laugh. "That's not bad at all!"

Goat-eyed Dustin approaches us slowly with open arms and exposed palms. "Hey, guys! It's okay. Really, it is okay. How about you come upstairs with us and let us take care of you—"

"Cover your ears! He's employing one of his incantations again!"

"Goddamn. I hate warlocks!" Savage says, practically wrapping his arms around the sides of his head in an attempt to block the mystical words from entering his brain.

"What the hell are you guys doing?"

I turn around to see Erik standing in the doorway to the triage unit with a thick neck brace on. He is drinking from a juice box. His eyes are still slightly rolling around in his head—a consequence, no doubt, from the massive head trauma he sustained less than six hours prior. He sucks the straw slowly, almost as if it's taking every last bit of strength to syphon the juice into his mouth. He closes his eyes, clearly falling asleep only to jarringly reopen them a split second later. "Wait, what?" he says with a chuckle.

"For the love of all that is holy, Erik. Please do not argue with me on this! These fucking sheep are trying to take us to the mental ward, where they will hook our brains to a piece of classified CIA technology to remove our inner wolf and reprogram us to be sheep. And we will be forced to sleep away the NIGHTS because we will be so utterly afraid of the dark! Long days of mild content just nibbling grass! Just waiting to die! Do you want that? We must go now!"

"He's out of juice!" he screams to nobody behind him, turning his whole body in the direction he wants to look, giving him the dexterity of a cardboard cutout. He aims back at me, still sucking the gurgling juice box. "Where'd she go?"

"She?" I turn around to see Savage hammer-punch a security guard right on the crown of his fucking head, shattering his face shield. The wallop sounds like a dubbed-over sound effect. It's so loud and over-the-top. It immediately turns the rent-a-cop's legs into wet noodles. His face goes blank like a computer screen turning off, and he falls to the ground.

A nurse calls for a gurney.

From behind, two of the guards grab Savage's arms. He wastes no time and starts charging backward, smashing them hard into the wall behind him. There's a crunch! And it doesn't come from the wall.

Patients whistle and cheer like spectators.

Savage pops up behind the fourth guard. The poor bastard never even had a chance. He suspects the unruly patient is close but loses him. He can't see! His shield is fogging up, so he takes it off to see. And that's when Savage brings his massive dick-beaters together, boxing the poor schmuck's ears.

Dustin is now casting spells on the PA system. "Code Violet. Emergency ward. Repeat. Code Violet. Emergency ward."

Two more guards arrive.

"That's it?" Savage shouts. He then bends down and, like he's picking up a puppy, scoops an unconscious security guard off the ground. "Ahhhhh!" he screams, hurling the flaccid guard at the pair, and it's almost cartoonish the way they get thrown back in unison, disappearing through the double doors behind them. Savage looks at me. "GET TO THE CHOPPER!"

I am unnerved by the collective insanity the warring nature of life itself plays upon people during daylight's regime; true horror is my visual arrest.

Despite all the blood and how it soaked into his long hair and how, in that thick and sticky black wad, the wound had appeared, upon initial inspection, considerably worse. In fact, two of the responding nurses could've sworn they saw actual brain matter exposed, which they made a point in relaying to the attending physician. Moments later, however, this proved to not be the case when a large section of hair was shaved from the back of the head.

"Erik! You got to wake up!" I slap him in the face. And when his head droops down, I scream at the sight of pale skin and thick-crusted maroon geometry etched in his scalp.

Twenty stitches and 800 mg of ibuprofen later, as the boys were getting provisions from the bus, Erik, with his rock and roll charm, will manage to coerce a curly-haired nurse into getting him a large quantity of narcotic that, when he takes, will begin compounding the effects of the concussion. Which is why when Classic Nick runs into triage to retrieve him off the bed, he instead finds him passed out and lying on the cold floor.

"Goddammit, Erik! Wake up! Wake up! Want some heroin? Come on, buddy! I'm ready to finally do heroin with you. Let's go and get it!" I grunt. "WORK WITH ME!" He falls, and I give him a kick to the hip.

Classic Nick struggles to successfully hoist up the deadweight, but after two more fails, Classic Nick, in his daytime stupor, manages to get Erik up and over his shoulder. "Let's go, buddy!"

Erik begins to wake up, utilizing neck muscles. A bash to the back of the head from the passing doorframe immediately puts him back out. Classic Nick steps out into the lobby where two parked cars (hospital security, no doubt) are parked right against the outside of the automatic doors. The doors are blocked, and now there's even more light with the high beams.

"Jesus Christ!" I shield my eyes. "Good Lord, that is bright!"

"No way out, hippie! Put your scrambled boyfriend down."

"I'M BLIND!" I stop to rub my aching eyes. "Wait! Who the fuck you calling a hippie?"

"They said he was your boyfriend too," Savage says weakly, but I can't quite see him.

"I was ignoring that, thank you." I have no idea what I am doing at this point, just standing here holding Erik, squinting, and trying to use my hands to shield my watering eyes. "Savage, why do you sound *so low?*"

"They shot me."

"What!" I look down on the floor and see him lying there with bright red coming out of three points in his torso. "Holy shit!" I drop Erik, and he hits the ground hard. I hear some people laugh in the distance.

I run over to Savage; there's tears in my eyes. "Somebody get him a doctor!" I scream, my voice breaking. Savage groans as he tries to roll over. "No! Don't move, buddy! Someone is coming!" Tears are pouring out of my face. I look up at the vague shapes in the blinding light. "WE NEED A FUCKING DOCTOR!" I look back down at the blurred image of Savage and his wounds. "Stay with me!" Now more distant laughs. "I am gonna apply pressure to stop the bleeding!" I say. As I put my hand on the bloody hole closest to his heart, I am instantly met with a tickle on my palm. I immediately let out a high-pitched "ooh!" and draw my hand back. "The fuck?" I look at my palm. Nothing. "Huh?"

Then the high beams turn off, and despite the massive floaters bouncing around my field of vision, I can see again. Before me is a whole mess of hospital security. I don't see the goat-eyed pair anywhere, but that's when I notice Dr. Zeus, and he's standing next to some Croc Hunter wannabe douchebag in dark cargo shorts who is aiming some kind of long gun at me. I pluck a red plume out of the unconscious Savage the same time he rolls over and farts a small gust in my direction, and then the Croc Hunter lookalike fires his gun at me.

Rape is the feeling of it going in! Crickey! The long snakebite, that one fang in the neck. Feels like a tire being slashed, but I'm the tire.

My x- and y-axis compress in on themselves as the old TV goes out. While I am under, I have the strangest dream about fucking Massachusetts. We are at its funeral—and by *we*, I mean, of course, Erik, Savage, and myself. Fuck'd for Life, as we happen to be. We were dressed in monkey suits and reading over the lowering coffin, which contains the fucking state of Massachusetts. Then at some point afterward—*next day, same day, who fucking knows?* It's the same dream!—an attic ghoul spits in my face a mouthful of my fucking father's blood and semen. It's an *old-world* message in the ghoul community that communicated, in no uncertain terms (a fact I just divined out of nowhere, mind you), that my father was met with a very bad and violent end that included some degree of rape by a supernatural who then stored in his cheeks both blood and semen for an inordinate amount of time. Weird, right?

*****

Intermission—I will not remember the Croc Hunter guy. Maybe blame it on the chemical drip-drop released into my body by way of FOREIGN BODY, or it's a shortcoming arising from my own foibles. Either way, I will not remember him pulling the trigger. I will *falsely remember* it was done by either one of the goat eyes (doesn't matter which to me). I will remember it distinctly, that one or the other (doesn't matter *which one*) stole our fucking tranquilizer from the Blunderbus and incapacitated me.

End of intermission.

*****

Soon after all three members of Fuck'd for Life are unconscious, the gags are removed from the mouths of the wild-eyed Dustin and Devin, both of whom are thrashing in restraints and harnessed on gurneys, jabbering on about losing control on black ice.

They both were telling this dreamlike story (but more so Dustin), conveying this wild tale about a Zamboni (or two) they were possibly driving together that was spinning out of control because of a "tribe" of hyena hockey players that spoke with a stereotypical mobster dialect. "Italian icemen" who slap shot spells at people they call evil magicians but who "are actually warlocks themselves."

"Schmucks clearly are on the same drugs we found in Patient Worthley's bloodwork."

Of course, nobody paid them any mind. The triage nurse, Janean Bruno, misheard their bad-trip narrations. When they said "black ice," she thought they said "black guys" and, disgusted, immediately issued that "these idiots be vocally subdued." She scorned—or better yet, screamed—over their psychotic blathering for the next forty-five minutes about their lack of integrity and how their current payrate of $6.50 an hour is more than they deserve."

They will also be admitted to the psychiatric ward.

*****

9/12—For the rest of the day, nothing as dramatic happens. I mean, aside from Dustin and me getting sectioned, no shit. And naturally, I mean, once we settled down and shit. I know we were obnoxious as all hell, but we were clearly suffering from a bad trip. Don't forget we were the victims here! We got Mickey'd, for fuck's sake. Next cat that offers me Italian ice is getting popped in the throat and shit.

Zeus told us to use the time to get to know ourselves. He told Dustin and me to journal every day. Any detail that comes to mind. Try to end it on something positive if we can. He said that twice.

I don't feel much like doing this no more. There's a whole book and shit I can write about today, but I'm going to pass out. It's 15:46, and I am spent. My brain's egg has been fried.

*****

I come to early Monday morning to a Hungarian nurse with nine fingers shaving off the rest of Erik's hair. It's so early, you could say it's late Sunday. It seems they put us in the same room. Pick up on the sarcasm when I say "yay!"

Immediately, I realize Erik will surely have a different personality now that he's bald. He must. Your personality is determined by your most recent haircut or hairdo. Or maybe it's deeper than personality. Maybe reality. It's like he's been rubbed by an eraser. One of his eyes is still remaining dilated, but now that it is set in his peeled potato of a head, it kind of makes sense. Jesus fucking Christ.

When I ask the Hungarian nurse what's going on with his eye, she shrugs and says, "I work here for twenty years, and I have never seen before." She pantomimes a finger across the neck while blowing raspberries. Then she walks out. She doesn't even clean up the hair!

I have a hard time returning Erik's void gaze now that he looks like a plucked chicken. He grabs a handful of hair and stuffs it in his mouth. I lie back down and pull the covers over my head and try to go back to sleep, but he begins to grunt incessantly—which, soon enough, turns into some half-retarded form of gorilla sign language with him demanding I read a book to him.

*****

9/13—Finally came across the ass pyrates today at breakfast and morning group session. Well, two of them. The fag goth of the two got his hair chopped for his upcoming brain surgery, I'm told. So I hope they forget a scalpel when they seal his potato head up and shit. And the gorilla is locked away in the dungeon and shit. You know what that means. Wink-wink!

Dustin started telling the other bag of shit patients here about how they drugged us, which made us appear as if we were having an episode. But fucking crazies don't understand reality and shit, so now there's this crazy rumor/myth spreading around the ward that we are under their spell and shit! I am not going to lie. That drug, for reals, fucked us up. Feel like my mind has been hijacked.

Focus on rest, routine, and therapy. That's 90 percent of what they stress here.

The doc and the nurses do a good job at keeping us apart. Good thing because Dustin is planning to kill them. He even showed me a piece of glass he plans to use to cut their front man's throat. Maybe I shouldn't be writing this. Ha ha! But it's true. Wouldn't want this journal to get in the wrong person's hands. Fucking mental patients are retarded, believe me!

I hate this place.

*****

I love this place!

Savage is kept in the "secure room" at the end of the hall with the blinking light, no joke. And they actually have him in a restraint jacket! It is fucking hilarious! And because he can't feed himself, his PADDED FUCKING CELL has a setup similar to a hamster cage, with a gravity-fed tube thing that dispenses him "NUTRITION Paste." That's what the label on the side says. I shit you not!

I wish I had a camera. I should bribe the fucking nurse to run to CVS and grab me a disposable one or something. The door to his room can only be opened on the outside. So I like hunkering down under the window of his door to fuck with him, whispering through the jamb, *"The devil is behind you! Turn around! The devil is behind you!"* And of course, the fucking goon starts going apeshit in there! It's a laugh riot! The height of comedy.

This place may be a shitty hospital, but I daresay it's starting to feel like home. I even managed to get some saucy Italian broad into the shower with me. That's really the only place where we get an extended window of privacy here. She has a fat ass like a rare T-bone steak that I put my fucking fangs in so deep, I almost took out a chunk. Maria is her name, and permanent residency here is *her game*! And she was bleeding like a machete victim. I sucked her cunt dry. Thick period gravy like I never tasted before. *Bloody Mary. Bloody Mary.* I said it aloud, and she came all right! Where's Savage with a rim shot when I need it? Only after did I find out she wasn't menstruating. No. Apparently, she was miscarrying. She says it happens all time since the doc rapes her almost every night, and her womb is as inhospitable as a fucking iron maiden.

So that's one for the books! See what I'm talking about with this place? It's like Christmas every day here. I should really talk to the doc about doing endorsements.

To top it off, I was even able to play one of our CDs for the patients here, which was very cool. They loved it! We just acquired a whole hospital wing of new fans! Just like that! And they are great. Really passionate people. Spiritual even! They love chanting and praying to all sorts of things, mostly electronics like remotes, thermostats, and televisions—which I know Zeus doesn't like. When they pray to false idols, he sends them to the basement for electro-shocks, so fuck him. Freedom of religion. These bastards are crazy, sure, but they need hope. I'm not a fucking missionary or anything. I don't care what you believe. God bless America! But I've been trying to hip a few of them to save their worshipping for the moon. I mean, we are in a fucking LOONY BIN, for Chrissakes! There's probably no better place to do it! It's a State-funded holy temple!

Savage hates it here. He doesn't mind the daily bouts of brain lightning. It actually seems to be having some wild reaction to his hair. I swear, it's not just the fact that he hasn't been able to *"buzz it"* lately, but I think the repeated electrocution of his fucking head is making his hair thicker and giving it more volume. He's looking good. Add to that the fact that he doesn't eat anymore, so his face is thinning out, and his cheekbones are getting more pronounced.

Funny enough! Whatever pills they have Erik on is making him eat all the time! So say goodbye to his abs. Fucker is getting fat now.

Naturally, Savage just misses the freedom. I understand that. The daily dose of wattage being shot into my brain can be annoying, but as far as vacations go, this ain't bad. I'm serious! People love bed-and-breakfasts. So on the surface, I'd say this is just as good; but here, there's community. We tell stories and talk about things that matter. And we try to work on ourselves, and I am starting to dig the idea of a *bedtime*! Not to mention a lot of these bastards are actually crazy, so there's always a level of unpredictability with the place!

We are thriving off our freedom. Of course, he can't go to the bathroom by himself, and there's no toilet in his PADDED FUCKING CELL, so he is constantly pissing and shitting himself. But that ain't nothing new with this bastard, especially after a few drops of the butter and a liter of tequila. *AM I RIGHT?*

But this is the fucking loony bin! There is piss and shit everywhere!

*****

9/14—That faggot goth threw a fucking pillowcase full of hot shit at us today!

It got in my eyes and mouth and shit! I think, somehow, he knew— or they knew—what Dustin was planning! 'Cause while we were on the ground squirming, trying to get diarrhea out of our eyes, he took the piece of glass from Dustin and ate it! Like chewed and swallowed the whole thing! They can't keep us here much longer! We work here! We have a good insurance! We have rights. We don't belong here. How does the doc allow this to happen?

I can't close my eyes without a thousand images of hideous growling fangs entering my brain and shit. So I can't sleep. And when I do, Dustin thinks I'm melting or something, so he wakes me up by shaking me. Violently. He only sleeps during daylight now because that's when he says the laugh of the hyenas are the quietest.

What the fuck is happening to us? I feel like this is happening worldwide right now. Not just here. Top it off, every mental midget here now thinks if they pray to the goddamn moon, it will save them! I told the asshole here—the one that looks like a genie—I told him to tell the fucking moon to get me out of here. Then I'll be a faithful servant.

*****

So admittedly, Zeus is the worst part of my little vacation home here.

He's always fucking here too!

Fucking annoying, the doc, always with the questions nonstop. Spouting gay fucking facts, he tells me to pay attention or he'll plug my brain back into the wall socket again. I flip him off when he's not looking. Do I know what *derealization* is? *Clinical lycanthropy? Alcohol-induced psychosis?* Blah blah blah. Shut the fuck up!

Dr. Fucking Zeus. *So obtuse. I wanna execute with a noose and set his patients fucking loose.*

He asks me if I know who Syd Barrett is.

"Yeah. I know who Syd fucking Barrett is!" I shout.

He flips the on switch, and a lightning bolt blasts through my head. I hum the lyrics to "Ride the Lightning" as he tells me shit I already know.

"Syd Barrett was another sick man like yourself. With dreams of rock and roll stardom. But because of an extended period of LSD abuse, he lost all of his sanity. And then that budding flower of a musical genius was cut short before it had time to fully bloom under the sun."

And when he says "sun," he blasts me with another bolt of lightning.

I am starting to think ol' Zeus is zapping me so I will give it to Bloody Mary that much harder later. Like a surge of electrical power lying dormant in me, just waiting to get out. I'm not joking. He knows I'm fucking her. Hell! We have to get *his permission* to be able to shower. He's the one with the key, ya know, because the showers are locked. Maybe not. I think the zaps are fucking with my brain a little.

Actually, you know what? I am remembering it correctly. Suck it! He's definitely been charging me up and letting me have a go at her! But why?

"But why not?" she says, bending over in the shower. This is whatever fucking time now. Later. Who cares? The important thing is it's nighttime. Living for the night will always be the only thing that matters. That and I've received my jump start during daytime hours. I'm buzzing.

She angles her juicy dago ass even farther, and with the way the water falls down her back and off her bum, it is like watching orange juice or beer commercials pouring deliciousness in fantastic slow motion. I can't help but squeeze her ass, then cup it. And I want to feel her pulse. I want her stink on my fingers.

She looks at me and bites her bottom lip. I look at my hand and see the reddest blood you have ever seen in your life. "You don't want to fuck me, *Papi*?"

I've been primed. My dick is purring like the seconds hand on the atomic clock.

"Whoa!" I say, putting my hands up. Then I smile. "I didn't say that!"

"So what's the problem?"

"Why is he allowing me to fuck you? When you said he's been keeping you prisoner here, preventing your release so he can keep on raping you, right?"

She smiles, clearly turned on. "Mm-hmm."

She goes to lure me in with a kiss, but I extend my hand. "Wait. Just a second."

She pulls her face away, crestfallen. Then she gets animated. "I don't want to wait. I want you to *cum in me* again."

"This isn't weird for you?"

She's getting annoyed now. "Dude, get over it! The world's a rapey place. So what?" She's breathing heavier now, and I think maybe the shower's gone cold, but there's clearly still steam. "Life is rape!" she says, poking me in the chest at the same time. "Get used to it, buster!"

I shake my head. "I don't want to."

Thank God for steam. Christ. *Steam!* I think of the polar bears. Then I tell Bloody Mary—*Maria*—what I'm thinking. "You know the guys that chill in a sauna for a while then immediately jump in ice water?"

"Okay?" she says, now choosing to step in the shower with me. "What's the point?"

"Point is my friend was raped by a couple of polar bears when he was young. Throughout the course of the night. Taking turns. Raping him in the ass."

"Oh Jesus."

"Yeah. Now he has a hard time with relationships."

"I can imagine."

"Well, think of it this way. His first sexual relationship was all over the place. *Hot! Cold! Hot! Cold!*"

She doesn't know how to react. She shoves me. "Fucking prick!"

I say "what." Then blood! And now this blood is the reddest blood I have ever seen, but it's not coming from her bottom half this time.

I recognize that look in her eyes from Erik. The empty gaze of head trauma. She went and slipped and bashed her head.

Or maybe that's just the look of empty trauma.

Something about Humpty-Dumpty comes to mind.

My following dream: I'm in the shower with a bloody Jesus, and it's very naked and very aggressive. Definitely gay, for sure! But I don't know if it's consensual. *Dehumanizing.* Let's just put it this way. If he likes it, what I'm doing to him, then no wonder his father killed him, okay?

The point of the dream was that I ate him afterward. After I *fucking came in him*, I turned into a dragon and chewed him in my mouth a bit, then literally ate the body of fucking Christ.

After raping Jesus, there's a smash cut, and he is now dressed like Elvis in a rhinestone jumpsuit while crooning "The Ballad of John and Yoko."

I think I'm awake now and strolling down the hallway of our favorite psych ward. A blond nurse with a power smile hands me a paper cup filled with a shitload of colourful pills that I will eat one at a time like a modest popcorn eater as I wave at the patients leaning against the walls. I am the grand marshal of the crazy parade.

I walk by the room of a patient, some crazy bitch named Evian (yes, like the bottled water), who has clearly taken a shine to Erik. He is sitting on the bed next to her and staring off with a completely transfixed yet detached gaze. I pause a second and suspect that he actually painted eyeballs on his eyelids, and he is, in fact, sleeping while she prattles on, which would be hilarious. This *half empty* crazy twat not realizing the asshole she's trying to fuck is actually unconscious wouldn't surprise me at all. Albeit he does drool a lot now, even when I know he's awake. I will give her that much.

Eventually, I do see him blink, and for some reason, it makes me laugh, which, of course, gets her attention. She flips me off as Erik looks around, almost as if he has to continually reestablish his present setting. I laugh again (then break the fourth wall). "Are we really that different?"

Elvis/Jesus gives a strong finish to his song as the crown of thorns lying atop his pompadour dig into his scalp, and blood starts trickling more and more down his forehead until it's like a full-on opened faucet pouring arterial red down his face.

I realize now that my POV is that of a camera, and I am *watching whatever all this is*. I may be in some strange in-between world. Think purgatory, for example. Or somewhere betwixt being in a medically induced coma or drug-hungry somnambulance.

I then watch myself get carried off by two orderlies to a secure room opposite of Savage's where I audibly begin to fret that this is, in fact, real life. Whatever that means. Inside, they fix me into a strait-jacket, and before exiting the padded cell, the larger of the orderlies takes a moment to knock me on my knees and give me a quick couple of slaps to the face. *One! Two!* I angrily scream *"ow!"* at them a couple of times as they leave. They say nothing. They just glare as they shut the door.

The camera pulls out of my space, passing through the tiny window in my door through the tiny window across the hall in Savage's door, and suddenly, I am in his room. I hear him groaning and straining before I see him. And when I see him, he pops into view. His hair is much longer now. *Impossibly long.* And he is wrestling to get out of the jacket, even tugging at the corner with his teeth. There are tearing sounds and shit as he is glaring at me/you with vicious intent.

We then pull away, back to the path, steady down the hallway until we ZIP in on Erik, where the Hungarian nurse and a doctor—not that awful bastard Zeus but another doctor—are giving him the rundown on *the brain surgery* he is scheduled to receive in a couple of days. He does not speak or react. He just stares out the window as raindrops begin to fall.

The camera goes through a couple more walls, and now we are in Primary Operations Room A, where most of the crazies are holding hands and praying to the moon. Those goat-eyed cunts are screaming at them to stop, but they don't. They keep chanting louder, and it becomes revealed they are repeating what the genie-looking patient is reading from that Robert Eisler book, *Man into Wolf: An Anthropological Interpretation of Sadism, Masochism, and Lycanthropy.*

In the course of it, men disguised as cats, lions, wolves, hyenas—formerly by the appropriate pelt, now by means of garments painted to resemble animal skins—work themselves up by ritual dancing into a frenzy that enables them to tear to pieces with their bare hands living kids and lambs and to lacerate the victims with their teeth.

The genie pauses and skips ahead a few pages.

On the basis of all these observations, it seems legitimate to describe recent man— *Homo neanthropus*—as a crossbred species. We are all descended from males of the carnivorous lycanthropic variety, a mutation evolved under the pressure of hunger caused

by the climatic change at the end of the pluvial period, which induced indiscriminate, even cannibalistic predatory aggression, culminating in the rape and sometimes even in the devouring of the females of the original peaceful fruit-eating *bon savage* remaining in the primeval virgin forests.

Little do the patients realize that a hurricane is working its way up the coast from the Bahamas. And Rhode Island, along with most of New England, is on its hell path, and officials are telling citizens to take necessary precautions.

"Who said that?" I shout, looking around my padded cell. "What hurricane?"

Meteorologists are predicting high winds and heavy rains, especially for the areas closer to the coast.

"I AM NOT KIDDING! WHO IS SAYING THAT?" I scream. It sounds like a woman narrating or something. And not just *any woman*. It sounds like English Black Dahlia, if you want to know the truth. Why the hell is she telling our story?

The camera POV is now looking directly at me, and I can see the answer. Clear as night. I smirk and think to myself, *We've got to get the hell out of here.*

The frame then transitions to a split-screen effect, where me and the boys each get a third of your screen. It's something you would see in a Brian de Palma flick. I shout, "Erik! Savage! Can you hear me?" And sure enough, they turn their heads toward my frame.

Savage screams back, "Yes! Yes! I can hear you!"

Erik makes a grunt that sounds like it is in the affirmative and starts laughing.

"Guys!" I shout, my voice cracking from excitement. "We need to escape! There's a hurricane coming, and that's our chance to get the hell out of here!"

Savage shouts, "How do you know this?!"

"I don't know! I think we are in a *time warp* or something like purgatory. Maybe it's hell? You know how Erik used to say that Satan had time-travel abilities. Maybe that has something to do with it!"

"Or," Savage says with a strange calmness in his voice, "maybe the world does end on New Year's, and this is reality *uncoupling* before the screen goes blank!"

"Maybe! Honestly, your guess is as good as mine! Or maybe we've been binging on some really *brown acid* this year, and we really have lost our minds!" I laugh, snorting at the same time. "Either way, we have to get out ASAP!"

Erik reaches his hand into his drawers, scratches himself, and then pulls out his hand and smells his fingers.

"Don't worry!" Savage says as he slumps against the wall. "The next full moon is on the twentieth. We'll transform that night, and then no one will be able to stop us!"

"No! No! No!" I say urgently. "We can't wait that long! They're planning on giving Erik brain surgery in the next few days. God knows what they will find in there. And who knows what will happen to him? And if they find something *unusual*, who knows what they will do to us? Ship us off to some underground military research lab to study us? Fuck that! This hurricane is our only move!"

Next Chapter

9/15—Hurricane fucking Floyd is heading right for us. The loonies are rejoicing and acting like this was a result of their crazy moon worshipping and shit. Time to batten down the hatches and shit. I think something is going to happen tonight.

Thus wrote goat eye. His last known journal entry.

*****

The boys and I petition the Boss to unleash our inner selves. Damn the harvest moon. We can't even see the Boss with this storm.

The crazies in the next room are scream-praying in a silly made-up language that kind of sounds like Latin. They begin stomping and clapping as if they were listening to Queen or something.

Tearfully, I plead to the spot above the storm clouds—the soft glow where I know the Boss is—and beg for what seems like hours to forgo waiting for the new moon on the twenty-fifth. Let us transform now, goddammit.

I say, "If you don't, we will really be Fuck'd for Life."

Then something happens. Moonbeams.

"'B' Movie" by Gil Scott-Heron starts playing.

It's split screen again. You ever see the music video to "Run, Joey, Run" by David Geddes? Doesn't fucking matter. Just know this: all growth hurts.

My bones crack. Pop. Shifting under the skin that's fading in colour and looking brittle. I scream to Savage in the next frame. His face looks like a pencil being swirled out by an eraser. He screams and the light bulb in his cell explodes. That's when I hear Erik's voice. It's calm like spring mist. And now his frame is coming from up top and pushing Savage's and mine to the bottom. Why does Erik get a full frame?

I hear Erik's voice in my head. "Who's in there with you, Class?"

There's a figure in my room now—in the corner, leaning against the protective padding, shrouded by darkness. In my heart, I know that he too calls the moon "Boss." I see now, in the weak light, that the man is bald.

"Satan?" My voice is weak from the pain that's radiating through my body.

He laughs. Then a gruff voice emanates from the mystery person. "Actually, my father named me Jesus Christ, but that's not important now." He crouches down, rubs his bald head. "What's important now is if you are willing to take this to the limits, just know there will be no going back. Do you understand?"

I am slithering on the padded floor. There is a revolution happening in my body right now. Sweat is pouring out of me. I stop groaning long enough to croak out a trembling "yes!"

"You understand you will be leaving humanity behind?"

"Yes!"

"You speak for your bandmates too?"

"Yes!"

He laughs again. "Very good! I love a fellow rock 'n' roll terrorist who also refuses to be tamed." He stands back up. "As the god of fire in hell, I wish you boys happy hunting."

And just like that, the man I called Satan disappears.

"Shoot, Knife, Strangle, Beat, and Crucify" starts to play, but fuck coming from moonbeams. I feel it coming from my soul! And now the pain is tremendous. It presents itself as familiar, something you've known your whole life or at least you thought you knew, but that knowledge is a fallacy. There's a whole world of pain out there to get lost in, and in that aspect is how it is like the moon. Something you've seen nearly every day. It has grown familiar, and you're even bored of it, but truth be told, you've only seen the bright face of it. Because let me tell you, there is a whole other **dark side** that you will never know because you cannot fucking handle it.

Chaos. Violence. And the Revolution.

As it turns out, I can barely handle it. The pain seems to last a *short eternity*. Brain feels congested with razor blades. I can hear my blood boiling. My bones are reshaping to that of my supernatural totem. The same is happening to Savage. I can hear his screams.

Of course, neither of us were surprised at the other's transformation. We are pyrates. We're bandmates. We have a metaphysical psychic link that kind of works like split screen or three-way calling, and till the end of time, we will always go down with the ship! Together! In fact, we took a minute to briefly celebrate our new and true forms.

"Erik! You laughing, vicious, demonic psychopath! You are CHAOS. Of course, you're a hyena!"

"Savage! You are the epitome of VIOLENCE. You're totally a fucking minotaur! Makes so much sense!"

Then all eyes are on me. Erik telepathically says, "You're the front man. An apex predator!"

Savage says, "You were always the best at howling at the moon! You are a natural-born werewolf, Mr. Classic Wolfe. A walking, talking, fucking horror story!"

I am REVOLUTION.

I was overcome by emotion. I think we all were. We teared up and embraced. I extended my hand out, palm down. The boys joined me, putting their hands on mine. "Better to burn out…than to fade away!" And we tossed our hands in the air. Time to get out of here. We started our way down the hall together, to the bloody end, till the ship goes down.

You know why? Because we are Fuck'd for Life, and rock and roll is here to stay!

The Boss was sending music down via moonbeams again. The soundtrack to our big escape. "I Swear" by All-4-One was playing loudly.

Power was mostly lost in the hospital due to the storm. Some emergency lights were on, but it's not like it mattered. The psych wing was in utter pandemonium. Fucking loonies were running around naked, throwing handfuls of shit into the doctors' and nurses' faces.

The genie set a pile of scrubs on fire. Then an orderly. That was funny, seeing a living fireball with legs running down the corridor.

A patient, some crazy broad with a Hannibal Lecter mask, was dancing with a dead security guard. Maybe he was unconscious, but he definitely looked dead. We tell her to come with us. We are getting the hell out of here.

"Okay, Boss!" I say, looking upward. And even with the storm and the hospital's roof between us, I now have the ability to see the Boss's face at all times, shining through. "Play something with some rock and roll!" I say, adding a howl.

The Boss winks. And then "Roadrunner" by the Modern Lovers starts playing, and we laugh and holler and high-five.

A couple of the suicidals take advantage of the chaos and tie an extension cord from the ceiling around their necks. We exchange a salute with them right before they make the plunge.

Red emergency lights are flashing. More fires. Sporadic puddles of blood. I step on a severed nose that tickles my feet a little bit. There is the constant sound of glass smashing. The Hungarian nurse comes out of a room with twelve or so scalpels sticking out of her solar plexus, and when she coughs up blood on the floor, I bend down to slurp it up as she keels over.

That's when that patient with the eyepatch, who is here for necrophilia, runs up to us, pointing to her. "You guys got dibs?"

We gesture with exposed palms, surrendering. "All you, buddy!"

He cackles, clearly giddy, as he drags her by her feet into the closest room.

Before he shuts the door, we hear him exclaim, "After a long day, I love cracking open a cold one!"

We tell him if he hurries, he can make it to our bus before we leave.

The patient who says he's possessed by 666 demons is levitating off the ground. His eyes are rolled back, and he's chanting in a deep voice. We high-five him as we run by.

I say, "Plenty of room to spin your head around on our special-needs bus if you want to get out of here!"

The Siamese twins with multiple personalities ask us if we can accommodate all of them.

"One seat?" I say, laughing. "Sure! No problem!"

The old lady who was diagnosed with pyromania after setting her house on fire asks us if we have any matches on the bus.

"The only match is your face and my ass!"

She grimaces, mumbling obscenities and quiet threats about setting us ablaze.

"I'm just kidding, you old bitch! We have plenty of Zippos on the bus! Come with us!"

We pull down our scrub hospital pants, and fully aroused, we chase down the goat-eyed bastards, taunting them with growls and demon laughs, all the while shouting, "SURRENDER YOUR BOOTY!" Even Erik is laughing like a spaz. We corner them in Operations Room B.

"Dead Moon Night" by Dead Moon starts playing.

Devin, his goat eyes welling with tears, shouts, "Fine, you faggots win! Just tell us how you managed to slip the LSD into the hospital food?"

The boys and I exchange puzzled looks. "What do you mean?"

Dustin, sniffling, points an accusatory finger at us. "You faggots planned this escape this whole time, drugging everyone here with your goddamn brown acid! Don't deny it! How did you do it?"

Did we? I mean, sure. Maybe one of us surreptitiously dropped some acid in the coffee. Or maybe one of our fans works in the kitchen and added some *butta* to the food?

"Or maybe, just maybe, we have done so much goddamn psychedelics this year that our auras are infused with reality-altering energy that ripples outward."

"Yeah! Ripples outward and affects the scenery around us kind of like…"

"Kind of like how the heat signature of fire warps the imagery behind it!"

"Fuck yeah!"

The boys and I high-five again, our exposed cocks bumping together. There's an awkward pause, and then we laugh and pull our scrubs back over our hard-ons. We play along with our air instru-ments to—what's playing now? "Aneurysm" by Nirvana. Yeah. We jam to that, unaware that the goat-eyed duo jumped out the large windows until we hear the *splat!* down below. We look down to see their hospital gowns being blown up by the hurricane winds, and we see both bodies in an expanding puddle of blood and their pale white asses aimed up at us.

"Sometimes ol' bastards would rather die than surrender their booty. I'm going to miss them."

*****

Savage bonks old Zeus on the head and hoists him on his shoul-ders, and we lead the mass exodus out into the parking lot in no time. The winds are intense. Rain is coming down like a madman (pun!), and it hits the skin so hard, it stings.

Erik looks at me and Savage. Then with his mind, he says, "I am done with normal rain now. I am all about *acid rain.*" And the three of us burst out laughing.

We run to the Blunderbus and pile everyone in. The keys are still in the ignition, and we take off.

There was a moment of reverence when Erik opened up a suitcase of his and pulled out three clean red skeleton jumpsuits he brought as extra. Savage and I rustled his still-growing mohawk on his large hyena head and praised him for thinking ahead.

"Minotaur!" I shout once we are cruising. "Take us to Providence Place Mall. We can wait out the storm in that secret room in the parking garage your artist friend is moving into. We will be safe in the parking garage."

"10-4, Werewolf! 10-4! Indeed!" he says as Hyena and I take long swigs from the laced tequila bottle. And then we pass it to Savage, who chugs from it as he inserts in a mixtape. "No More of That" by Stiff Little Fingers comes through the speakers, and we thrash and dance down the center aisle of our special-needs bus that's filled with escaped mental patients.

We waited out the storm in the mall's parking garage, although we couldn't find that secret space Savage was talking about. Didn't matter really. There wasn't anybody there. Obviously. Who the hell shops during a fucking hurricane?

Anyway, I will say traveling with crazies definitely gets old after a while, especially when they go without much-needed medication after a couple of days. And I have to say, they shit and piss a lot. Even more than Savage, which I didn't think was possible. Not to mention, they suck at partying because they are always sleepy. None of them liked tequila or acid, and most of them bitched when we put on any loud music. I couldn't wait for the Boss to tell us to eat, which didn't happen until the genie started taking down our Jolly Roger, saying that "he didn't much care for pyrates." That he was more of a cowboy guy.

Fucking cowboys? That's right. When the boys and I heard the Boss's voice, it was a one-word command: "Feast."

I have to say, I rather enjoy killing and eating people. For any of you out there who are contemplating such actions, I cannot recommend it enough. It's freeing, empowering. I think I like it more than playing music. If only I could do both at the same time, that'd be the dream.

But seriously, if you are on the fence about taking a human life and then eating the meat from their corpse, stop worrying. It's the fucking twenty-first century! Nothing means anything anymore! Just do it! Sin is an antiquated notion. Who gives a shit! Do you have any idea how horny you get when you use your teeth to rip the throat of a fucking human? And a crazy human at that.

I joke with the boys that we have to be careful. You know, "you are what you eat." I made that joke a lot, actually. We laughed. We listened to the album *Funhouse* by the Stooges while we did it. Remember, it's fun to listen to music, get drunk and twisted, and laugh with your friends. *That* should be the title of our autobiography. Shit. In the book, we can give pointers on how to kill people and eat their flesh. That will be the overall theme of the book—that killing people is the height of entertainment. We can end the last chapter with *"We don't know if eating a victim's heart is art, but boy, do we sure like it!"*

It will surely sell a billion copies.

I will say the secret to killing someone: go for their eyes first. Blind them! Not to mention, they are delicious. And now that they are without sight, their fear cranks up to 11, and any predator knows fear makes the meat that much tastier.

I should also note here that now that I'm a full-time werewolf and have, in fact, personally killed and eaten…what…at least four of the loonies myself, I will say—and this will definitely excite all of your religious folks out there—that there is, in fact, a soul. It exists. I know because I've tasted it. That's another ability werewolves like myself are endowed with. We can taste and consume human souls. It tastes like a quail egg, and in fact, it's also good for our fur.

I even ate some brains for the first time. It was the genie's. I cracked his skull open with the ghetto blaster and, with my claws, got in there and ripped off a sizeable chunk of bone. I think brain is now my favorite food. Don't get me wrong. I liked eating that bitch's miscarriage. I thought that rejected baby batter was delicious, but now that I've eaten brain, there's no comparison. Plus, it's exciting to know you are devouring someone's personality and memories. So between that and the soul, it's almost as if I am consuming their whole life. And now they don't exist and arguably never did.

Ha ha ha!

We didn't kill all the loonies. Erik and I bit a few of the cooler ones—the Siamese twins being one of them (or two?)—and let them go be were-whatevers. We set them loose in Rhode Island. We are in the monster franchise business now! Savage the minotaur didn't bother trying to infect any of them because the bite of a minotaur ain't communicable. He ain't WERE. Erik and I jokingly chastised him by gesturing Ls on our foreheads for "loser" and saying "moooo!"

Ya know, because he has a bull's head.

We saved Zeus for last. Savage bit off his fingers one by one as I held him down and Erik put on his strap-on dildo and, using some of the loonies' blood as lubrication, raped him while we played "Leng Tch'e" by Naked City. He's kind of an old man, so after the first five minutes, it was like shoving your fingers in the hole of a jelly donut and moving it around frantically, meaning his fucking booty lost shape real quick. He sobbed loudly, which we thought was pretty gay. Erik ignored this, of course, and kept assailing him with the strap-on. It sounded like a leather boot being stuffed into a raw turkey. His body didn't last very long after that, and he kept crying, which was fucking annoying, and praying to God, which I found to be disrespectful since he knows we be moon worshippers here, and this pyrate sped bus is our church.

"You boys don't have to do this! You boys are sick! Very sick! You are not experiencing reality! This is all in your heads! THIS IS ALL IN YOUR HEADS!"

Then he said something about us having advanced stages of rabies or some such nonsense. I don't know. I couldn't listen to him anymore, so I grabbed a handful of nearby viscera from the floor (or seats, for that matter) of the Blunderbus (we are messy eaters!) and shoved it in his mouth.

Fifteen minutes and fifty-one seconds into the song, when the vocals of "Leng Tch'e" start up, Erik pulls the strap-on out of his pro-lapsed asshole. Savage starts gnawing the tip of his dick while I rip his balls off. I tried eating one, but it tasted like metal, and I threw up.

Last Chapter

There we were, real-life monsters taking the stage dressed as red skel-etons. We finally made it back to Massachusetts, rejoicing when we saw a sign that said "Welcome to New Bedford. We've been expect-ing you!"

We stopped at the first shitload club we could find. It was some hole-in-the-wall in the city's south end called "The 13th Floor." When we took the stage, I immediately screamed nonsensical end-of-the-world prophecies into the microphone regarding the new millennium.

"The universe is in a state of dispassionate uncoupling! We are the harbingers of the apocalypse! Satan has a time machine, and we are monsters who take orders from the moon, and we have declared a holy war against reality!"

During our set, we frolic onstage like demon spawn. People shout at us to take off our masks, and we shout back, "This are our real faces!"

On stage, we play all our much-loved classics. At one point, Erik pulls out his greasy hyena cock and pisses on some retard with large ear gauges. Then right after, Savage shits in his hand and chucks it into the crowd. They get uppity and start throwing bottles at us, but we hold our ground as I shout at them, "You should be praying to your scrawny Christian deity, hoping that we keep playing music, or else we'll come down there and start gobbling all youse up! You are food to us! We will turn youse into shit! WE WILL TURN YOUSE INTO SHIT!"

All things quiet down for our last song as we pull out our acous-tic instruments for the soft little gospel number I wrote on the ride here. "For the next song, we're going to try something a little differ-ent than we are used to."

> *When your pale moonshine casts down*
> *upon me! I feeeeeeeeel like I'm in the brightest*
> *spotlight in the wooooorld!*
> *Shine down upon me your ancient wis-*
> *dom! And in retuuuuuurn, I will set fire to*
> *this woooooorld!*
> *Well, I accept your challenge, Mr. Boss*
> *Moon! And just for yoooooou, I will devour*
> *these sheep all niiiiiight!*

Then the tempo speeds up and the tune gets a little circus-y.

> *They will feel your might. No flavor quite*
> *like their fight!*
> *It's out of sight! Maybe tooooooniiiight—*
> *I will kill for a thrill or just to chill your*
> *spine—*
> *And just like that! Your soul is mine!*
> *Then to cause you more strife, I will kid-*
> *nap your wife to ensure she's fuck'd for life!*

And there they go, horror-movie monsters on a psychedelic crime spree.

We spend a week driving from town to town, causing havoc and living under the codes of conduct the Boss demands.

In Dartmouth, we sneak into a random country house in the middle of the day. The pictures on the wall suggest a dopey husband and a fat wife live here with their two bullshit kids. We use almost three fucking fluid ounces of pure liquid LSD to spike all the bever-ages (except the beer) in the refrigerator. Around midnight, we drop off the homeless man we found the day before in downtown New Bedford talking to himself and chasing people in the parking garage with rusty scissors. We tell him, "This is your house now! We got it for you! Anyone else here is just a demon!"

He nods in agreement and heads to the front door. All the while, crying kids and female screaming can be heard on the second floor. A light turns on, and we hear a dopey voice say, "There are no monsters!"

We give the homeless man a thumbs-up just before kicking in the front door. We peel off while "Moon Upstairs" by the Dictators plays.

Cruising down I-195 E, we drink hard from the laced bottle. "Codeine" by the Barracudas is playing quietly as we discuss how some of the best movies ever made had someone die on set:

1. *Top Gun*
2. *The Twilight Zone: The Movie*
3. *The Crow*
4. *Gone Fishin'*

"*Gone Fishin'*?" This was, of course, put out there by Savage. The douchebag.

Erik gives him an incredulous look, and because he is still nonverbal, Erik, since the escape, has been consistently practicing his telekinesis. So since the start, he's been able to direct his communications to both of us simultaneously. And now when he starts focusing on Savage, who isn't reciprocating his glance because he is driving, I assume they are engaging in a form of private communique, so I gracefully bow out and cast my attention elsewhere. I turn and look out the window up to the sky and look at the Boss, who is staring at me with a warm intensity. I smile, open the window, and howl.

"*Heeelp meee...*"

I turn to see Savage panicking. His hands are off the steering wheel and fumbling at his throat. "*He's choking me!*"

I look back. Erik's got the beginnings of what will become a large evil grin on his terrifying hyena face.

I slap him on the side of the head without using my claws. "Erik, stop it! STOP IT! He's just a big fan of Joe Pesci!"

"I'm a wrecking ball. I'm an atom bomb. I'm a night terror. I'm a nuclear sub. I'm a weapon of mass destruction that's controlled by a loose toggle switch.

"I'm an asteroid. And scientists believe I am what actually ended the reign of the dinosaurs."

Blaring "Society Is a Hole" by Sonic Youth on the ghetto blaster, Erik and I crash a movie theatre in Cape Cod after setting a fire in the lobby. After running out the emergency exit, Savage backs up the Blunderbus right against the door. The smoke seeping out gets thicker as the wailing from the other side of the door gets louder and more frantic.

I shout, "What? Can't hear you. What's going on? Is there an emergency? Can you repeat that?"

Savage, smoking a cigarette behind the wheel, smiles and exhales smoke out of his bull nose as Erik cackles his hyena laugh and plays "Clip the Apex…Accept Instruction" by the Dillinger Escape Plan.

Afterward, we pop more acid and drink more tequila.

"The moon is not just a god, he's the best god! Working for him is such a treat! For he commands us to eat all the human meat!"

We do more of the liquid LSD, basically two shots a piece, then chase it with a handle of tequila. We go back to Boston and spend a whole night listening to Ween and killing neighborhood cats. We have to stop several times to jerk off as we keep getting boners for whatever reason.

A werewolf with a bottle of tequila. A were-hyena self-administering LSD with an eyedropper. A minotaur thumping his fists against his chest. They speak to the moon that doesn't talk back as they play with their butterfly knives and quote Nietzsche.

Back in Worchester, we angrily stab a deformed guy in a wheelchair like fifteen times. His blood comes out like a whisky pour. I guzzle it like it's mama's milk. And again, there's more erections, and again, we take care of them. Inside the cripple's fanny pack, we found his address, an army man, and three Tootsie Rolls, which we promptly eat.

"God, I haven't had one of these in a while."

"No kidding!"

"Did you know they make strawberry ones?"

"Is that right?"

"Wouldn't lie to you."

"I should definitely try that sometime!"

"I think you would like it!"

"Ya know what else we should get some time? Pixy Stix!"

"Oh, hell yeah!"

"I haven't had a pixie stick in forever!"

"I used to put them in my Cheerios as a kid."

"No shit. Me too!"

"I'm lethal. I'm fatal. My favorite delicacy is prenatal. I should have been aborted. I think procreation is a sin. I'll eat a living baby, even my own kin."

"The Lord Is a Monkey" by Butthole Surfers is playing.

We debate whether to bring the cripple back to his house for his family to find. None of us want that meat. Erik suggests we dress him like a scarecrow and leave him on the lawn of his house because, surely, he's someone's dependent. Savage says we should set him on fire and roll him down the street. And when we do finally set him ablaze, Savage heaves the troll down a modest incline of a somewhat secluded road. You'd expect him to go hurtling with a fantastic speed like some celestial fireball destined to inflict some faraway destruction, but even in death, the troll is a disappointment. And after ten feet, the shit-goblin tumbles out of his wheelchair. The flames extinguish, and he's just lying there in the middle of the road, smoke rippling off him while a wheel of his capsized chair winds down, much like our dwindling excitement.

"Fuck it," I say nonchalantly. "Let's eat the runt."

"I'm a hand grenade that bursts all colourful like fireworks.

"I'm a kamikaze pilot without a plane, always crashing into the lives of strangers just for sport.

"I think tomorrow we'll go terrorize children at parks with fire. They're sixty months old, and it's time to abort."

In Fairhaven, we go to a titty bar called *Temptations*. With the promise of fast livin', we pick up a few of the stripper whores, but their attitudes change once they come aboard the Blunderbus and see the putrid pools of coagulated blood collected in the aisle and the rotting remains of the loonies sitting in the back seats.

The head bitch, the olive-complexioned one with large amounts of sex-pulp in her ass and tits, gags and covers her mouth. "Is this a joke?"

Minotaur takes a quick bite out of a small human hand he keeps in his pocket. "It's the Kill-ennium. Isn't everything a joke?"

"Halloween joke!"

We tie them up and make them drink our soup, hot water and dirty syringes we've been collecting all over the state. We dissolve a bottle of Flintstones vitamins in the batch and tell them it's good for their hair and nails.

We force them to fuck a couple of the dead loonies. We lie and tell them we won't kill them as long as they give it to them good. We lie and tell them once they cum, we won't stab them in their stomachs and have sex with their wounds. We lie and tell them we aren't sacrificing them to the moon for a lifetime of moon powers. We lie and tell them that we love them.

Hyena's now doing heroin. Minotaur starts a cycle of steroids.

"Am I the only normal one here?" I shout as I stab some pimply teen in a skate park for not being able to name seven Iggy Pop songs. I am stabbing him with a sharpened femur bone, naming a song each time. "Nightclubbing"! (I stab him in the kidney.) "Some Weird Sin"! (I stab him in the other kidney.) "'The Passenger"! (I get him in the lung.) "'Lust for Life'! Come on, motherfucker! You don't even know 'Lust for Life'?" I look at him lying there in a pile of blood, dying and crying and being a lame-ass sheep.

"Jesus Christ, werewolf! Look at him. He clearly doesn't know anything about having a lust for life!"

We set like a dozen cars on fire. It's "Goodbye Sober Day" by Mr. Bungle playing all the time now. We put metal ball bearings in the paintball gun and fire at people coming out of hospitals and places of worship as we scream the name of the song "Goodbye Sober Day." We kidnap that nun and give her some butter and tell her the devil is always right behind her. We set houses on fire too. We really like fire. The moon does too. The Boss gets off on the smoke, gets high from it. And it bellows into the atmosphere, and he inhales the smolder. We laugh and cheer him, and you know he's proud of us as his eyes mist up.

> *"But the tour is over. It's time to grow up.*
> *"We need to mature and accept a life of being mildly complacent.*
> *"That's why we are heading back home to see our girlfriends* (The boys join in for this part.)
> *"WHO WE KEEP PRISONER IN OUR BASEMENT!"*

After the song, we smash our acoustic instruments that are filled with blood and viscera of those we killed. We TWIRL their intestines, splattering vivid COLOUR all over the goddamn place.

****

I believed it to be the end of November when they returned as I was doing my best the whole time to keep track of the days. But I later learned it was actually the thirtieth of October when we heard their godforsaken "Blunderbus" pull up to the house, "The Boys Are Back in Town" by Thin Lizzy blaring on their stereo.

Time makes fools of us all.

We've evolved so much that by the time we got back home to our red house on Mulberry Street in Springfield, Massachusetts, we doubt the ladies will recognize us. We unlock the metal security door that leads to the basement. I think there is a toothpick or a bobby pin in the keyhole. Clearly, those foolish cunts were trying to "pick it" and escape. I point it to the boys, and we share a laugh.

They clobbered down the stairs; our hearts were in our throats.

"Honeys, we're home!" I say in a singsong voice. "Don't be alarmed at our appearance. You wouldn't believe the trip we've had!" I see the TV is still on as we left it.

They smelled awful. Like vinegar, booze, cigarettes, garbage water, and the pungent odor of rotting meat. Their eyes conveyed total madness.

They are covered in dried blood.

Savage says, "Totty baby!" He holds out his arms. "I sure have missed you! I wish to fornicate with you at once. Come here! And please don't mind my *bullheadedness!*" he says, laughing, and a little smoke comes out of his nose.

We are fixed into our animal forms now. Permanently. Never to play human ever again.

Totty, who, this whole time since they left us down here, has remained, for the most part, mute. Becca too is clearly in shock as to our situation and maybe even catatonic. I comforted them the whole time, whispering in their ears as I played with their hair that everything would be all right.

Totty extends her arms and, in a daze, starts making her way to him, but I jump in front of her. "Back the fuck off, Savage! You stay away from her! You stay the fuck away from us! All of youse!"

I look at Erik, who looks like his body is unaware he died a while ago. His eyes are vacant, and he looks like shit. "Erik! Help me! You said you loved me! So help! Also, what the hell happened to your hair?"

The three of us laugh and look at each other. I say, "Listen, sweetheart. Erik had an accident, and now he's essentially retarded. Well, a little retarded, but don't think of him as lesser in any way. He can still fuck! But yes, he is largely nonverbal now. I mean, he still laughs, but that's really it. He can communicate with us psychically, and I don't think that would work with humans."

I scratch my furry face. "And as you can see, he is a were-hyena now."

Erik starts sending me a telepathic communication.

"Oh, what's that, Erik?" I hold out a claw to English Black Dahlia, signaling *one moment*. "Oh, I guess the Persians call were-hyenas *kaftars*. New to me. I never heard this." I shrug and pause as he clairvoyantly says more. "Oh, he says that the Ethiopians call them *budas*." I flash a professional smile and point to Erik. "See! Still full of useless information! Same old Erik!"

I cough. "You know. More or less." I turn to Rebecca. "My dear, I am sorry for not calling you on while we were gone, even though I said I would, and which is why we got youse that phone," I say, pointing to the buttonless one-way telephone we got for the basement before we left. "I think I was nervous about the idea of finally being *official* with someone." I snort and chuckle. "Ya know what I mean?" I give her whole body a scan. She is pale, crying, and staring off. "Sweetheart, what's the matter? You look like you lost weight. Are you feeling okay?"

I get loud. "No, she's not fucking okay! Neither of us are fucking okay! You fucking sick assholes drugged us on some bootleg acid, ditched us downtown while we're having a bad trip, and then youse ran around town doing God knows what! Then the next morning, after we drove your fucking sped bus back here, you fucking psycho losers fucking grabbed us, GANG-RAPED *us, and locked us here in your dungeon of a basement for over a fucking month! The windows were boarded up and cemented over, so we haven't seen daylight in forever! Do you have any idea how crazy and anxious and depressed you get when you don't see the sun? Fuck you! No! We are not okay!"*

All three of the broads are weeping now. Jesus! Everyone's a diva when it comes to sunlight.

Savage, who is a minotaur now, takes a moment to adjust the thick metal ring through his bull nose, then asks, "By the way, are either of youse pregnant after that?"

"No, we are not fucking pregnant! If we were, we'd use a coat hanger and abort the fucking demons!" I yell at them then spit at their horrible faces. "Fucking psycho retards!"

"As it turns out, the three of us are, in fact, actually open to the idea of having babies. And we'd like youse to germinate them." He laughs and, with his human hand, rubs the side of his bull head. "I guess you can say we did a lot of growing while we were away on our trip.

"And yes, Totty-honey, I am a minotaur now. But don't worry. We are still pyrates."

"Fucking minotaur?"

"Yes, of course!" I say as I turn away from admiring my wolf-face in the now broken *Coors Light* mirror on the wall. "We will always be pyrates! It is, after all, a life philosophy. And yes, Rebecca baby. Unlike the boys here, I didn't evolve into anything else when we were channeling the words of…what's his name, Erik?" I pause, waiting for him to tell me with his brain. "Oh, that's right! Robert Eisler! Duh! We were channeling his beliefs about humanity and our violent and sexual bestial side and how we are likely to end all human life from inevitable nuclear war. And we are trying to escape that fucking looney bin without the aid of the full moon, and he was right! It worked! The power was in us the whole time!

"The Boss is always there, and he is always giving orders! The secret is having the ability and the focus to *listen*! Tall order these days, huh? Going back to nature! To our roots, right? With our fast-paced lives, the worldwide web, and all our gadgets, but we did it! And instantly, we transformed into the forms we hold now before you as this is permanent! But that's a good thing, Rebecca! Life is just like playing an instrument. The goal is to get better! To ascend! To evolve! And yes! I am still just a simple werewolf."

I get down on one knee, and out of my pocket, I pull out the ring, which I forgot was still on that bitch's finger. I pull it off and toss the finger, giving a nervous chuckle. "Oops." I clear my throat. "But this simple werewolf now knows what he wants. Rebecca, my sweet! I have grown so much, and I credit that, marginally, to you. But I have so much more to grow, and the important thing is I want to do it *together*. So here I kneel before you and ask you, Rebecca… uh…whatever your last name is. Will you do me the honor of becoming…*Mrs. Wolfe?*"

I ask this, and at the same time, I am looking again at the broken Coors Light mirror and thinking how it looks like several large shards could have been extracted from it. But who would purposely break a mirror? Isn't it bad luck to break a mirror?